ABOUT THIS BOOK

Fact One: A flock of crows is called a murder.

Fact Two: Cherophobia is the fear of fun.

Fact Three: It's impossible to sneeze with your eyes open.

For Sedona Mathews, facts and knowledge act as a buffer between her and the outside world. Born as an empath, others' emotions bombard her senses, complicating any relationship she's tried to enjoy. When she becomes sole owner of Shelf Indulgence, she happily devotes her life to the Havenwood Falls bookstore, hiding away amongst books she loves. Because there's another fact Sedona is painfully aware of . . .

Fact Four: In a town where nothing and no one is as they seem, falling in love can be treacherous.

Micah Westbrook has no time for love. Cloaked in secrecy, he brings his niece, Holly, to Havenwood Falls, hoping they can hide amongst the other supernaturals. He's charged with keeping Holly safe and will risk everything to ensure those hunting them can't pick up their trail. The last thing Micah needs is to be blindsided by a danger he didn't see coming . . . Sedona.

Micah struggles to keep her at arm's length, forgetting one important fact: When it comes to loving an empath, there's nowhere to hide.

NOWHERE TO HIDE

A HAVENWOOD FALLS NOVELLA

BELINDA BORING

To my late father-in-law, Donnie Boring.
You are loved and you are missed.

CHAPTER 1

You can do it, Sedona. There's no need to panic. Everything will be okay. Just put on your big girl panties, smile, and pretend that you can't feel everything he is thinking.

If I had a dollar for every time I'd rehearsed this small mantra, standing here at the window of my bookstore, Shelf Indulgence, I'd have enough to leave Havenwood Falls and explore the world for the rest of my life.

Not that I truly wanted to leave the only place I'd ever felt safe enough to call my home, but you get the idea.

I sounded like a broken record that kept skipping and repeating the same old tired words. Part of me wished I could toss aside my reservations each time I decided to bravely face the possibilities of dating.

The problem was there was nothing normal about beginning a new relationship, especially when you held the special gifts I did. My mother used to tell me how unique being an empath was, and that when my ability was paired together with my other inherent powers, I would become a force to be reckoned with.

Those pep talks ended by the time I reached my teens, replaced by the now familiar fear that echoed in her heart. She was careful to prevent it from ever shining out through her eyes or filling her voice when she spoke. I didn't need those nonverbal cues to know what she was feeling.

The empathy I'd been raised to believe was a gift morphed quickly into a curse—one that kept my peers at arm's length, their soft whispers following behind me as I walked down Havenwood Falls High's hallways. I didn't blame them for not wanting to invite me to sit with them at lunch or bond over fun sleepovers.

Even though many of them were part of the hidden supernatural community, somehow their fangs, claws, and weirdness weren't nearly as dangerous as being able to reach into them and pluck out their secret feelings.

It wasn't until I found comfort in running Shelf Indulgence and escaping into the beloved books I cherished that I made my peace with who I was—am.

"I could always cancel," I murmured, my stomach churning with nerves. "It's only a first date . . . nothing important." My throat dried the second I spotted Robert crossing the street, headed in my direction. "God, I hate this."

A deep, familiar voice answered. "One of us needs to leave this store and have a life, Sedona. And considering I can't, that leaves the burden firmly on your shoulders."

Maxwell appeared beside me, his fingers twirling the end of his mustache. I often wondered if he realized he did that—if it was a nervous habit he'd failed to break. I couldn't quite cross out an alternative thought that it was his way of impersonating a villain because right now, my dearest friend wasn't enabling my cowardice at all. He was supposed to agree wholeheartedly with me and suggest I spend the evening secluded quietly in my apartment with a delicious glass of wine and a book.

"I still think you made that up, Maxwell. I'm sure if you tried hard enough, you could leave and go haunt Willow over at Coffee Haven. You know . . . expand your horizons and all."

A look of horror and disapproval blazed across his ghostly features.

Did I forget to mention Maxwell was a ghost?

"I'll pretend I didn't hear you suggest that, young lady. Do you really think I'd stay here and witness your weekly neurotic diatribe about the woes of dating if I could simply waltz out of here?"

I knew Maxwell well enough to remember that beneath his offended pout, he was teasing me. Like he said, we pretty much went through this conversation each time I foolishly agreed to go out with someone. We both had our parts to play.

Clenching my hands into fists, I straightened and drew in a deep breath. "How do I look? Am I presentable enough?"

Despite my blasé attitude toward dating, I still found myself making an effort, a small sliver of hope surfacing that maybe, just maybe, this time would be different.

"You look beautiful as always. Although," he paused for a moment, casting a glance outside as Robert drew closer. The corners of his lips twitched into an almost smile. In stepping off the curb, my date had misjudged the slickness of the ground, his feet slipping over ice. To some, winter in Havenwood Falls was far from the magical wonderland that I viewed it as. Robert's mouth formed a silent curse word.

Maxwell cleared his throat, bringing my attention back to our conversation. "I believe your beauty is wasted on this human."

There was no mistaking the sneer in his tone. My dear friend didn't approve of my dating someone outside our supernatural community.

"You know why I agreed," I retorted, steeling myself to once again remind him that there were slim pickings for me no matter how hard I tried.

Who would want to date an empath?

"Heathens," Maxwell exhaled in disgust. "In my day, men would be lining up around the town square for a chance to be with you."

"Well, pity we can't just hop in a time machine and find me these rare males." I laughed, desperately hoping it disguised the sadness I couldn't always bury. Truth be told, I was lonely. Just once, I wanted to experience the toe-curling, heart-racing, giddy swooning love I read about.

My gaze remained with Robert now—the moment I'd been

waiting for. The closer he came, the sooner I would sense his intentions. Over the years, I'd become pretty good at protecting myself from the overwhelming crush of emotions that surrounded me. It was one of the first spells I perfected when I came of age and could practice magic on my own. Invisible to the naked eye, a silvery aura encased me, thinning only when I purposely lowered my guard to get a reading of someone.

He must've sensed I was watching because a huge smile lit his face when our eyes met. Everything seemed normal as his intentions mentally reached me—nerves over whether he could impress me, a list of topics to cover over dinner just in case we ran out of things to say, and that he believed I was one of the prettiest girls he'd ever laid eyes on.

That last one made my own smile grow. What girl didn't like knowing others thought she was attractive?

Robert was only a few steps away from the store's door when I caught the briefest of flashes of another feeling—one that instantly brought the shutters around my heart. Sighing sadly, I knew I couldn't forget and pretend he hadn't just cast aside those other emotions for one that made my skin crawl.

Lust. The lewd kind that left you feeling stripped bare and vulnerable in front of a group of men catcalling and yelling for you to shake what the good lord gave you.

I was far from being a prude, so lust in general wasn't something to make me retreat. There was nothing wrong with finding someone good-looking and noticing how they made your body respond.

That wasn't how Robert was feeling right now. If anything, he was contemplating how long it would take him to get me flat on my back, legs in the air, as I screamed his name in worship.

"Blech," I uttered, already heading to the door. "Be right back, Maxwell." Not giving him a chance to reply, to convince me I didn't have the luxury of turning yet another man down, or to list the million reasons he worried I would become the Cat Lady of Havenwood Falls, I was out on the street. I was the queen of excuses, and I didn't feel guilty for the lies I told Robert, or the fake

4

disappointment I expressed over having to cancel the plans he had for us.

It took everything I had not to shudder when he rubbed my arm, his touch lingering longer than was appropriate. Another blast of lust shot out from him, and I took a few steps backward.

I couldn't run back inside the bookstore fast enough, leaving Robert standing on the sidewalk, confused over how I could possibly choose something over him. His arrogance was another turnoff—something he'd managed to hide when he'd asked me out earlier in the week.

"What was the reason this time?" Maxwell asked, exasperated. If he rolled his eyes any harder, they would've fallen to the back of his head and down his body, before coming to a stop in his feet. Snarky ghost.

"Unexpected inventory audit," I answered weakly. Even I could hear what a lousy reason it was. "In my defense, he was a pig."

His brows furrowed in concern. "You can't keep doing this, Sedona. Do you honestly want to end up like me?"

"I could think of worse things to become." In trying to lighten the conversation and perhaps deflect the lecture I sensed brewing within him, I couldn't deny he had a point. "Next time I'll go, okay? Just not with him."

He snorted. "What was wrong with this one?"

My face flushed. "Let's just say, if given the chance, he'd rather have skipped dinner and dived right into dessert."

A deep baritone laugh burst from Maxwell. "He found you attractive and that upset you? You do know what happens when two people like each other, Sedona? Please tell me I don't have to inform you about the birds and the bees."

The very thought made me squirm uncomfortably. "I already know about sex, smart-ass." I shook my head at him. "I just don't like it when the guy I'm with is more interested in getting between my legs than really getting to know me."

"And here I thought I was the old-fashioned one," he retorted quickly. "You can't hide away in here forever, Sedona. Sexual sparks are a good thing. You need chemistry." His voice grew louder and more passionate. "The heroes in those romance books you love won't keep you warm at night. You need someone real."

"Says the ghost that won't leave either." It was a low blow, but I was feeling defensive.

In the years since I'd taken over my grandfather's bookstore and made it my own, I'd never once seen Maxwell leave. He'd simply appeared one day, and no amount of questioning would get him to reveal where he'd come from.

"My circumstances are different." His response was gruff. As an empath, I couldn't get a fix on his emotions, my gifts reserved solely for the living, but in this case, I didn't need to rely on my gift to know what he was feeling.

We were both defensive.

"I'll try harder next time," I promised, wishing I could reach out and touch him without my hand passing through. "He just wasn't right for me."

"You can't afford to be so selective. You need to seize the moment before time slips through your fingers. Take it from me." His voice trailed off.

It was on the tip of my tongue to ask him why, to perhaps prod a little to see if he would finally open up and share.

I didn't get the chance, however, as the door to the store opened, startling me. Maxwell disappeared, leaving me standing there like a fool, talking to myself. Most times that wouldn't bother me. Most of the town believed I was weird anyway, so nothing really surprised them.

As my heart began racing and my mouth instantly dried, all I could think was two things:

One, I hoped this guy didn't think I was a freak too.

Two, the stranger standing in the doorway, his gorgeous blue eyes fixed completely on me, was by far the sexiest man I had ever seen.

And when he spoke, I knew I was in trouble.

CHAPTER 2

"*H*ello."

They say that words hold power, and living in the small town I did, they could also be very dangerous. Witches used them to invoke magic, shifting energy through the ether in order to do their bidding. One wrong syllable or nuance could cause an outbreak of aggression with the werewolf packs, and vampires . . . well, they were notorious for using their silken tones to bend others to their will.

But this one word—hello—it had the power to completely undo me. I'd heard it countless times throughout the day as customers came into Shelf Indulgence, but never was the greeting connected to the man that personified sexy goodness simply from uttering it.

I gulped.

Don't you dare stammer and embarrass yourself, Sedona. Just take a deep breath and act as if it's every day a gorgeous stranger stops by to say hi.

I gulped, again, my palms already beginning to sweat from nerves.

"How can I do you?" I blurted out, instantly cringing over the jumbled sentence falling out of my mouth. Inwardly, I wanted the floor to open up and swallow me whole.

HOW. CAN. I. DO. YOU?

What the heck!

If I thought him speaking melted my insides, his laughter was pure sin. The twinkle in his deep blue eyes set me at ease and, despite the heat blistering my cheeks, I knew his grin was a sign that he had a sense of humor.

"Is that how you greet all your customers?" He cocked his eyebrow as he asked, and my heartbeat thundered.

This man was going to be the death of me.

"Only the good-looking ones." It came out all breathy. Then, as if the Fates needed proof I'd lost my ever-loving mind, I winked. *Winked.*

Awkward silence followed.

Even Maxwell showing up and scaring the bejeezus out of me would've been more welcome.

In the space between seconds, I automatically reached out with my empathic gift, searching for those telltale signs that he was one of us— supernatural. I hadn't seen him before, and perhaps he was simply passing through. Something in the back of my mind whispered that I hoped that wasn't the case.

Electric tingles brushed over my skin, setting those nerve endings aflame with magic. He was definitely supernatural, but what species? Each group had a certain flavor that belonged solely to their kind. It made it easy for people like me to uncover.

The Court of the Sun and the Moon often called on me with tasks to subtly dig into someone's psyche to see whether or not their intentions were true and honorable. Havenwood Falls was fiercely protected from unwanted attention, and although I didn't want to get involved with the town's politics, I couldn't resist my aunt's requests.

Just my luck. She knew that it bothered me, but didn't hesitate to remind me it was my duty as her niece and an empath to use my gifts for the common good.

Sometimes that line got pretty murky. I didn't like invading people's privacy and had spent years trying to master my own control.

After a hellacious childhood of blurting out people's emotions, revealing their innermost feelings without permission, I'd retreated into the world of fiction, where it was safe.

Characters I understood.

People were just . . . complicated.

I pushed outward again, imagining tendrils of light reaching toward the quiet stranger, who was now eyeing me with curiosity. I couldn't quite get a reading on what he was—my mind was fogging over and keeping the answer just out of reach.

Testing to see what feelings he was protecting turned up even more questions.

Nothing. He was the perfect balance of calmness, like a blank sheet of paper. If it weren't for the fact I could read his facial expressions and body language, I would wonder whether he was actually there.

It was tempting to push harder. I was inquisitive in nature, and this was a puzzle I wanted to solve.

Again something whispered that he was someone I definitely wanted to know more about.

Just as my innate magic touched him, a sizzle of energy snapped out, causing me to take an actual step back.

His eyebrow rose again.

Did he know what I was doing?

Covering my tracks in case he did, I cleared my throat and offered a shaky smile. "What I meant to say was how can I help you?"

There was a quick wrinkling of his brow before it smoothed over and he nodded. "I'm needing a book for my niece. She's studying history, in specific the Tudor era with King Henry the Eighth. There is a reference book she needs." Digging into his pocket, he pulled out a folded piece of paper before continuing, "*The Life and Loves of the Infamous King Henry Eighth.*"

Excitement fizzled up inside me. This was one of my favorite subjects to read about.

"Not that I condone putting aside reading for watching television," I started, making my way through the shelves to where I kept historical books, "but she may want to watch *The Tudors.*" It was on the tip of my tongue to gush about how incredibly swoony Jonathan

Rhys Meyers and Henry Cavill were in the addictive series, but I didn't think he'd appreciate the sudden surge in estrogen.

"I don't think that would be a wise parental choice, considering she's only fourteen." He leaned in, and I caught a whiff of the most delicious scent. Whether it was him or his cologne, I didn't know, but it took everything in me to move away.

"My name's Sedona Mathews, by the way. I'm the owner of Shelf Indulgence."

"I know," he replied in that deep baritone voice that liquefied everything. This reaction was beyond strange, because the only time I'd *ever* felt such a strong reaction to a guy before was when I was reading one of my beloved novels.

They were safe, however. He was not.

What I meant to say was "You do?" but what erupted out next was nothing short than a ridiculous squeak. A huge part of me hoped against hope that Maxwell had retreated to wherever he goes when he's not annoying the hell out of me.

With all the grace I could muster, I answered the only way I knew how.

"Did you know that King Henry was well known for how incredible his legs were? That's how men's beauty was described back in the 1500s. Apparently he had attractive calves."

Facts were my life. They brought me comfort in stressful moments because they didn't ever change. I'd heard some say the same about mathematics, which I thought was completely bonkers, but facts were like a lodestone I could touch and ground myself with. I kept them all filed away in my head on the off chance there would be a situation I could share them.

Like with this stranger.

And the king who had six wives, two of whom he beheaded.

I rested my hand lightly on the shelf containing the books about the English monarchy.

"Well, it would be ironic if he was known for having a beautiful neck, wouldn't it?" He placed his finger on one of the spines, mouthing the title silently. "My name's Micah, in case you were wondering."

I blinked. I seriously felt like some starry-eyed teenager in the presence of her idol. Shaking my head, I berated myself for not being more professional.

"It's a pleasure to meet you, Micah." Turning to face the shelves again, I scanned the section briefly and let out a disappointed sigh. "Looks like I don't have it in stock. When does she need it by?"

Micah was still studying the books, slipping a few out before returning them to their place. "Why?"

There was a flicker of emotion—suspicion.

"Because if you don't mind waiting, I can order it in for you. Shouldn't take more than three to four days." Thank goodness for Amazon shipping.

He seemed to ponder that for a moment before nodding. "I'm sure she'll make do with what she has until then. I've never seen anyone read as much as she does. Every time I turn around, she either has her nose stuck in a book or she's sharing what she's learning."

So she was a kindred spirit and fellow bookworm.

"How is she liking Havenwood Falls High?" I asked, guiding him back to the front of the store, where my computer was. He followed behind quietly, and it wasn't until I was typing in the web address that I realized he hadn't answered.

He was studying me with the same intensity he gave the books back there. It was almost like he was an empath too and was trying to push beyond the barriers I kept raised for protection.

But I hadn't detected that gift.

"Sorry." I offered an apologetic smile, and my hands paused above the keyboard. "I forget that not everyone is as nosey as I am. My mother told me that one particular trait would get me into trouble one day."

Micah's features softened. "You're fine. I'm just not used to meeting someone who doesn't seem to have an agenda." Before I could ask him what he meant, he pulled out his wallet. "Did you want me to pay for the book now or later when it comes in?"

"You can pay now." Accepting his card, I began entering the information into the computer.

"Do you need to see my I.D. as well? To make sure I am who I say I am?" He extended his driver's license out between his two fingers.

One look at his earnest expression and I shook my head. "I trust you. Besides, I know where you live." Smirking, I pointed to the screen where his order was still displayed.

"You shouldn't be so willing to trust strangers, Miss Mathews. Not everyone is so easy to read."

Damn, was that him saying he knew I was empathic? The hair on the back of my neck rose.

I decided to take a page out of his book and change the subject. "Is there a number where I can reach you when the book arrives?"

"How about I stop by at the end of week and check in with you? That might be best." Micah was already at the door. "Until then." And with a slight head nod, the most intriguing man I'd ever met was gone.

My fingers flew over the keyboard, the book for his niece ordered within moments. I let out a weary breath as I sat back on the stool I kept at the front counter and stared out at the town square outside. Micah had already disappeared from view.

"Well, that was interesting!" Maxwell boomed, his smile all teeth. "I must say I've seen you flustered before, Sedona, but that was something else."

"How much did you see?" I asked, knowing the answer already. The ghost had witnessed the entire thing.

"Enough to wonder what people would've thought about my fine legs."

A groan escaped my lips, and it was tempting to bang my head against the countertop. Why couldn't I be like everyone else and not embarrass myself at every turn?

"Cheer up, my dear. There is a ray of sunshine peeking out from behind those clouds of gloom." He gestured above my head like he could actually see them.

"And what's that?"

"You've got the next couple of days to rehearse what you can say to him when he comes back for the book. Perhaps you could study up on some American history facts to dazzle him with."

"Have I told you how much I hate you?" I retorted halfheartedly. The truth of the matter was he was right—my head was already ticking over what to say next. There was no way I would be caught off guard again.

"Maxwell," I asked, taking one last glance out the window, "have you ever met someone who you couldn't read, or heard of someone an empath felt little emotion from?"

"Usually they're people with secrets to hide. Why?"

I shrugged and put on another smile. "No reason. Just curious."

The rest of the evening passed quickly, but Micah was never far from my thoughts. While I usually honored people's privacy, there was something about him that I couldn't put my finger on, and I was determined to figure it out.

There was one thing I did know—when it came to my gifts, when I focused all my intent, there would be nowhere to hide.

CHAPTER 3

"*I*ncoming!"

Austin's quick-fire warning could mean only one thing.

Before I even had a chance to prepare myself for the approaching storm, the bell jingled as the door opened.

Thanks for the heads up, I mentally groaned, making a quick note to give the high school student a stern talking-to if I survived the next few moments. I loved Austin with all my heart. Hiring him a year ago had been one of the best decisions I'd made with regard to the store, because his love for learning rivaled my own. He also was a natural whiz kid when it came to computers. In fact, the current system we used was his recommendation. The kid definitely had his finger on the latest technology pulse.

Frankly, I'd have been somewhat lost without him, but I would never tell him that.

"Sedona." Her greeting was short and to the point. She glanced around the quiet store, a frown creasing her forehead. "I trust business is good?"

My aunt didn't bother to try hiding her disappointment that I'd eagerly chosen to take over my grandfather's beloved bookstore instead of following in her footsteps and working for the coven. She didn't understand how appealing a life surrounded by literature could be. Instead, all she saw was dust and shelves, pages upon pages of tedious reading. I'd spent many evenings desperately trying to help her see, to somehow help her feel what I did, to no avail. She may have been a witch, but she was no empath.

My mother had been one—a powerful one, judging by the stories others had shared with me. My heart hurt whenever I thought about all the many missed opportunities of being guided by her as my gifts emerged.

That was before the tragic accident that had stolen my father away from us. Within a few months, my mother had joined him—dying from a broken heart.

Love could be deadly for empaths.

"How are you today, Aunt Millicent?" There was no point in commenting on her original question. No answer would please her.

A black head of hair peered around from behind one of the bookshelves. The expression Austin wore as he mouthed *sorry* was almost comical. Part of me wanted to beckon him out so he could act as a buffer between us.

"Is there somewhere private we can talk, niece?"

It always amazed me how effortlessly my aunt could reduce me to a little child being scolded. With a long haughty glance around my store, I knew she was looking to see if we were alone.

"If you'd rather we talk in the back storeroom with my inventory," I stated, my heart already sinking with all the possibilities of why she wanted to have whatever conversation she'd planned away from prying eyes and curious ears. "Or you're more than welcome to come by tonight and we can chat."

Secretly, I wished she'd opt for neither and leave. Her unexpected visits were rarely meetings I cherished. That could be because the majority of the time I felt she saw me more as a pawn to do her bidding than as family.

While she didn't exactly enjoy the inner circle of the coven, we had ties to the Beaumont family, and she ranked high in the coven. She absolutely enjoyed being useful to those in power.

She let out a snort of disgust. "My time is precious. I'm sure your back room will suffice." Without waiting, she sashayed past me like she owned the place. "Better yet, send the boy out on an errand."

I knew better than to argue, because that would only result in her lingering longer. I loved my aunt and was grateful for the way she'd taken me in after my parents' deaths, but when she got this particular look in her eye, I knew this wasn't a social call.

I quickly dispatched Austin on a java run, telling him to take his time coming back. The instant flash of gratitude in his eyes spoke volumes.

She scared the crap out of him—something about how he was terrified she could peer into the deepest recesses of his soul or curse him to become a toad. I always chuckled whenever he said that, because what kind of secrets could a seventeen-year-old boy be hiding?

When I finally returned to her, Aunt Millicent let out a loud, overly dramatic breath. "As you know, coven business keeps me busy, not that I'm complaining." And here it came. "You know. Your gifts are being squandered in this . . ." Again, she didn't bother disguising the disdain she felt as she glanced about Shelf Indulgence. "Quaint little store. Why he left it to you is beyond anyone's understanding. He knew I had bigger, more impressive plans for you, Sedona."

With my parents dead, it had fallen on my aunt to continue raising me and seeing to my education—both academically and supernaturally. The obvious choice would've been my grandfather, but with his advanced age and reclusive tendencies, the task had been left to my mother's older sister.

It was my turn to sigh. "Did you really come here to argue, aunt?" I asked, feeling my own sense of sadness that she couldn't see how happy my life made me.

Sometimes feeling her emotions weighed on me like a concrete-encrusted blanket. It was suppressive and overwhelming. It totally eclipsed the bond of love and family buried beneath. It was *that* version of Millicent that I longed to be nurtured by.

She sniffed. "I only want what's best for you, my dear niece." A flyer on the front counter caught her attention, giving me a temporary reprieve. "What a shame. Heidi had so much potential. If they don't find her soon, I believe it will destroy her poor family."

My gaze strayed over to the photograph I'd memorized.

Heidi Bennett had disappeared during the Cold Moon Ball back in December, and no amount of searching had led the authorities to her whereabouts.

"Is there still no news?" I asked, genuinely hoping there were at least a few leads to go on.

Aunt Millicent shook her head and placed the flyer back with the others on the counter. She then turned her steely gaze back to me. There'd been a flicker of compassion there—of some long ago memory that had surfaced—but it evaporated the moment she started talking again.

"Can you not see why I push so hard for you to come work for the coven?"

I closed my eyes briefly, my shoulders sagging a little before I repeated the same words I always answered her with. "We all have our own paths to walk. This is mine." I stepped away, as if joining with the shelves behind me, my private comrades. "Why can't you see how happy I am?"

"Duty doesn't always equate to happiness, Sedona."

And there was the truth—the reason why I believed my aunt was so fixated in converting me over to her way of thinking. For her, everything was about duty and control. She was willing to sacrifice happiness, and even love, if it meant she held power and could be of use.

She couldn't comprehend that there was a myriad of ways of fulfilling your life's purpose that didn't result in being miserable.

"Was there something in particular you wanted?" It was time to focus on the real reason she'd stopped by the store. Aunt Millicent wasn't one for idle chitchat.

Her gaze narrowed, and her lips turned up at the edges in a half smile. "Can't I simply visit with my niece?"

I remained silent. We'd played this game many, many times over the years.

With a sigh of exasperation, she finally nodded. "Well, now that you mention it, I heard you had a visit from a newcomer yesterday . . . a Micah Westbrook."

Thank goodness she didn't share in my gifts, because the blast of longing and heat that coursed through me at the mere mention of his name would've shocked her.

"Yessss . . ." I drew out, cautious.

"What were your impressions of him?"

There it was, the reason why she'd come, and not because she felt any sense of obligation toward me as a family member.

She was fishing for information. Sometimes being one of the few empaths in town was exhausting. It made conversations like this a tangle of weird intentions.

"He seemed like a nice guy," I answered. "Why, is he of interest to the coven or the Court?"

Everything was about the Luna Coven, in my aunt's eyes.

"As you know, whenever someone comes to live in Havenwood Falls, they must meet with us and state their purpose. He registered when he first arrived, but the coven's High Council is still . . . curious." The way she spoke that last word sent an involuntary shiver up my spine.

"Something set off a red flag?" Unintentionally, I'd stepped forward as if being drawn into the intrigue.

The movement wasn't lost on her.

"You know I can't discuss the High Council's business with you, Sedona." There was a *but* in there somewhere. "But, while he appeared to be honest and upfront, there was something not quite right about him that they couldn't put their collective finger on."

Here it was.

The request I always dreaded.

"I need you to get a reading on him, Sedona." She quickly held up her hand to stop the refusal she knew was coming. "And before you get on your moral high horse, remember that you are my niece, and the position comes with certain responsibilities. While I barely condone you hiding away in this musty bookstore, I won't continue to support you constantly neglecting your gift. You were given empathy for a reason. You will do this task for me—and your High Council—without complaint."

"And if I find nothing of consequence?"

Her lips pursed. "I will be the judge of that. Do this for me, Sedona. Do this, and it will be last time I will ever ask."

It was the same promise she always offered and one I knew she'd never keep.

"He seems like a great guy, Aunt Millicent." I replied carefully, because while I believed he was hiding something, the last thing I wanted to do was tell her she was right. Once unleashed, my aunt could be relentless in pursuing answers. I needed to know for myself before I confirmed her suspicions.

She pushed again. "Is that all you felt? You didn't feel anything out of the ordinary?"

I shrugged, suddenly tired of this whole conversation. Why couldn't things be simple between us? "He was polite when he came into the store . . . perhaps just gaining his bearings as a newcomer."

"You will do this for me." It was more of an order than a request. She gave one last look at the missing person flyer. "For all we know, he's connected to Heidi's disappearance."

She'd found my Achilles heel. As much as I wanted to respect people's privacy, and regardless of the temptation I felt over uncovering why Micah was like a blank slate, I couldn't ignore this.

I finally relented. "Okay, one more time, and then you won't ever ask again."

The smug look of satisfaction across her face made my stomach dip. "Thank you, niece. The Council thanks you as well."

In a flurry of cheek kisses and a request for me to stop by on Sunday for dinner, she left me standing, staring out after her.

Fifteen minutes later, Austin reappeared, two large coffees in his hands. "Is it safe to come back?" Austin's whispered question broke through my daze.

"Yes, she's gone," I retorted, shifting slowly before turning around to face him. "You couldn't have warned me sooner? I thought we had an unspoken code that whoever saw her coming would let the other know?"

Austin's gaze dropped to the ground, softening whatever annoyance I felt. "There wasn't enough time, I promise." He walked over to the large bay windows. It would be time soon to change over the display. "So what did she want?"

I gave him a look that told him I wasn't going to be confessing anything anytime soon. "Just family stuff. Nothing that warranted the cloak-and-dagger routine."

This only made him laugh. "With her flair for the dramatic, she'd be perfect in the theater." Austin handed me my drink before taking the lid off his own and blowing across the heated surface. "Although God help the fool that hires her." He shuddered before realizing what he'd said. "Sorry, Sedona, I know she's your aunt."

That was the perfect cue to change the subject. "So, Austin, what's the word on the street?"

His eyes lit up. "Did you know there's a new girl in town? Everyone at school was excited to meet her, but she never showed up because she's homeschooled. Rumor has it she lives with her uncle in a house they're renting by the Kasuns'." The fact that this was his gossip reminded me that my young friend paid more attention than I gave him credit for.

But he did share something interesting. Micah was living out by pack property. I was surprised the alpha, who was also our sheriff, had okayed it without knowing everything about Micah—from a thorough background history to what type of toothpaste he used and how he liked his coffee.

"Makes sense that her uncle came in here looking for a book for her, then," I commented, finally moving to the computer at the front counter so I could check on the order status.

"He did?" Austin's eyes went wide with interest. "You met him? When will he be back to pick it up?"

My finger traced a line on the screen. "Looks like it should be delivered here in a few days. Perhaps I could drop it off at his home. It'll give me a chance to meet his niece."

"Uh-huh." His teasing grin told me he could see right through me. "Maybe I should join you, and then I can convince her to come to school. The drama department is always looking for fresh meat. Speaking of which," Austin's voice raised an octave in excitement. "You're officially looking at the recipient of a full-ride scholarship!"

All thoughts of Micah were temporarily forgotten. "You got it!" I squealed and threw my arms around him. "Austin, I'm so excited for you! What does this mean?"

"It means I get a free ride to any college I choose." He was positively beaming with pride. "I heard I was a shoo-in for it, but you know . . . there's always a part of you that reminds you of all the ways you suck."

"You? Insecure? Really?" I gently teased back. Despite the cocky confidence he seemed to ooze, it wasn't surprising that he also doubted himself. "I can't think of anyone more deserving." I quickly gave him a warm hug. "So will you be majoring in theater?"

His answer surprised me.

"I'll be minoring in it. I figured I shouldn't let my tech skills go to waste, so I'll be majoring in computer science." And with that, a huge toothy grin spread across his face. "You know, something to fall back on in case my career on Broadway doesn't pan out."

Suddenly a wave of sadness washed over me. "So you're leaving after you graduate." It was more a statement than a question.

Austin nodded. "As soon as I figure out where I want to go, I'm out of here."

Most supernaturals stayed in town and enjoyed the protection it provided. But with Austin being human, the world truly was his oyster.

"You do know that I shouldn't be too happy for you. After all, I've invested so much time in training you, and now I'm going to have to start that process all over again. You're pretty irreplaceable." I tried to look disappointed. I turned the corners of my mouth downward, but couldn't hold it. A smile quickly broke out and revealed my true feelings.

He had the decency to look at least a little remorseful. "I can ask around to see if anyone would be interested in replacing me. I could even train them for you." Austin's expression was one of pure earnestness.

"I'm just kidding you. It will all work out. For now—" I gave him another quick hug. "Enjoy your accomplishments and let me know a good time for us to go out and celebrate. This isn't something to ignore."

The rest of the day passed by uneventfully, giving me a lot of time to ponder the discussion with my aunt. As much as I hated it, she'd roused my curiosity once more.

I took one last look at the order screen before closing it out.

Mr. Westbrook, what are you hiding, and do you understand how much danger you're in now that my aunt's picked up a scent?

Chances were he was about to find out.

CHAPTER 4

$\mathcal{T}$he days seemed to drag on slowly. I hadn't seen Micah at all, and part of me wondered if I'd simply imagined the dark-haired stranger in my store. I knew I'd often been accused of having my head in the clouds, daydreaming about the romantic stories I devoured by the page, but he'd been very real. The order page I kept stalking by the hour proved that.

"Look what just came in," Austin declared, holding up a package triumphantly. "Maybe I should go deliver this, or better yet, we should call Mr. Westbrook and have him personally come to pick it up himself."

There was a muffled cough and chuckle from the back of the store. Maxwell had also taken to teasing me about my sudden fascination with Micah, something very unbecoming of a ghost his age. When I'd mentioned that, he'd grinned, rolling the end of his mustache between his fingers like some conspirator.

From what I understood, I was the only one who saw the store's deceased occupant. I considered that a blessing, because there was no way I could ward off both Maxwell's and Austin's digs at how flustered I became at the mention of Micah's name.

Austin's latest game was seeing how many times he could make me jump by mentioning the newcomer's approach to Shelf Indulgence. It was only when I threatened to fire him, or worse, make him do the next six months of inventory by himself, that he simmered down.

Snatching the parcel from his hands, I scoffed as if I truly wasn't affected by the book's arrival.

"Don't you have something to do? Shelves to dust? Someone else to annoy?" The more I spoke, the softer my questions became.

Carefully opening the package, I slid out the book. Yep, *The Life and Loves of the Infamous King Henry Eighth, Fourth Edition.*

"You're okay to watch the store while I run this over to the customer, aren't you, Austin?" I already had my phone and the book in hand as I headed toward the door. "If you need anything, you can reach me on my cell."

"You look fine, by the way," he called out after me. Damn kid was too smart for his own good.

"There's no way Austin knew where you'd go first," I murmured, looking about to see if anyone was watching before turning around and heading back toward the Havenwood Village apartments. It was stupid that I felt the need to hide what I did, but if there was one thing the past had taught me about living here, it was that you couldn't be too careful. This town was founded on secrets—whether you were human or supernatural. Someone was always watching, taking note of everyone's activity. While I had nothing to hide, it didn't hurt to show caution anyway.

One false move and you could be the center of your very own Havenwood Falls scandal, the town's chief gossip the ever-reliable ringleader.

"Sedona? Sedona, my dear, just the young lady I was hoping to bump into!"

Speak of the devil.

One moment the street was empty, and the next, Irene Beckett stepped out of Pyntz Butcher Shoppe.

Here was one other person, besides my aunt, who had a sixth sense when it came to anything newsworthy and hidden agendas. Irene currently stood in the middle of the sidewalk, forcing me to stop and acknowledge her.

"Hi, Mrs. Beckett," I answered politely, forcing a jovial smile across my features. She was the last person I wanted to see today. "How are you?"

In one sweeping glance, she took in my appearance, and her dark eyes twinkled. "I hope once you visit with the mysterious Mr. Westbrook that you'll stop by the salon and let me know all about him. He's quite the catch, from what I've been told, but way too elusive for my liking. I should've known he would've sought you out, my pretty friend." She reached out and brushed a stray strand of hair to the side of my face.

Did I also mention that she had absolutely no respect for personal space?

"How did you—" I began, before she spoke up and answered.

"Why, the book, dear." She pointed at the package I was holding. Without thinking, I raised it to my chest, hugging it tighter as though it was a shield that could somehow protect me from her scrutiny. "Tell me, what kind of books does he read? Suspense or mystery, perhaps." Irene paused long enough to catch her breath. "Something tells me a man like him would be more into works of nonfiction than fiction."

It was often hard to keep up with Mrs. Beckett, but even this made me laugh. "What makes you think it's for him? Seems you've given him a lot of thought."

She waved her hand through the air, dismissively. "Of course I would. While I'm no longer in the market for a husband, that doesn't mean I don't look out for my younger friends. In fact . . ."

I inwardly groaned over what I knew would pass through her lips. Taking a page from her own book, I held up my hand to stop her. "I can find my own boyfriend, Mrs. Beckett. I'm perfectly capable."

I took a step back, glancing around to see if anyone could come rescue me. Like a blessed angel of mercy, Callie stepped out of her consignment store for a moment of fresh air. She also scanned the street, and as our eyes met briefly, I wanted to scream for her to come help.

As if by magic, she nodded and called out. "Oh, Mrs. Beckett. I had some new items come in this morning that I think you'd like."

The town gossip looked back and forth between us, silently trying to determine which conversation she wanted to continue.

Please, go to Callie. Please, please, please.

She placed her hand on my forearm, gently squeezing it. "Stop by the salon later and fill me in on all the details, will you?" Before I could let out a sigh of relief and mouth a quick *thank you* to Callie, Irene added one more opinion. "And there's no need to hurry home and change. You look beautiful already, Sedona. He would have to have rocks for brains if he doesn't recognize that."

"I promise," I answered, lying through my teeth. Waving her off, I stood for a moment, my nerves rattled. I guess you could say that was one of Irene's special gifts as well.

Turning around again, I headed toward the address I collected from Micah earlier in the week. There would be no stopping home quickly to check my appearance. If I did, it would just add fuel to the fire, leaving Irene to gossip with someone else about me changing clothes to deliver a book.

"You're going to die a spinster at this rate, Sedona," I grumbled.

And the thought of that was more depressing than usual.

CHAPTER 5

One of the things I loved most about living in Havenwood Falls was that it truly was a gorgeous place. Set in the midst of lush greenery that still caught my breath in the morning, my childhood home was surrounded by beautiful, majestic mountains. If there were ever a place that could cater to the many needs of the supernatural, it would be this town. It lacked the constant hustle and bustle of larger cities, but the residents liked it that way. As it was, the many prying human eyes always seemed to be on the verge of discovering how closely they brushed shoulders with the supernatural.

Not that the humans we lived alongside were completely oblivious, but it was much easier for the Court to govern and watch over a small town like ours. As for me, I loved the quaint charm Havenwood Falls held, and while there were definitely times I wished I could be invisible and simply blend in with the crowd, the small population was less chaotic against my empathic nerves.

I'd carved out a piece of heaven for myself and didn't really see myself leaving. Taking in a lungful of clean, fresh air, I could feel the energy that often thrummed quietly around me gently caress over my senses.

Spring was coming. While each season held its own brand of

appeal, I loved watching the world wake up and the coming of new life
—the trees leaving behind the bareness of their branches as green
leaves flourished and flowers blossomed. The rivers and creeks would
grow fuller as the snow melted. Creatures would emerge from their
wintry slumber, and the days would grow longer and warmer.

Something inside me whispered that this spring would bring
something more personal and fulfilling than the picturesque scenery
waking up. A new feeling was brewing deep within my spirit—a
promise of growth and something I couldn't quite put my finger on.
All I knew was it caused butterflies to flutter in my stomach and a
pulse of excitement to quicken my breath.

Leaving the main streets of town, I followed the familiar path that
would lead me to where Micah and his niece were currently residing. I
was a little envious as I paused long enough to sidestep a heavy branch
hanging over the trail. Small snowflakes glittered onto my hair from
the pine needles above.

While I loved the magical feel of winter and Christmas, I was
ready to say goodbye to wet boots and cold fingers.

It didn't bother me so much today, though, and I knew it had to
do with seeing Micah. The man had taken over my thoughts and
refused to budge. Over and over, I relived our encounter, questions
filtering through my mind of possible reasons for him moving to
Havenwood Falls.

With his modest home finally in sight, those butterflies kicked up
a notch into a full-blown flurry and storm. My mouth dried from
nerves, yet I kept on walking, as though drawn to him like a magnet.

The books that I read described this feeling as falling in love, and
while I was a romantic at heart, being an empath had layered that
feeling with a healthy dose of practical reality. There was no such thing
as insta-love, at least not for me. Unfortunately, I wasn't some gorgeous
heroine being swept off her feet by some tall, dark, and handsome
stranger, and as mysterious as Micah was, I was pretty sure he wasn't
my knight in shining armor.

I swung the small wooden fence open and approached his front
door. With each step, my anticipation grew, and for the briefest of

seconds, I prayed that he wasn't inside. I was being a coward. Yes, I often felt uncomfortable around people and would much rather be back in my bookstore with a cup of hot chocolate and my nose in a book, but life was about risk.

As scary as it was for an introvert like me, it was good to step out of my comfort zone. Besides, it wasn't like Micah was a werewolf or vampire. He wouldn't be biting me anytime soon.

Rapping my gloved knuckles against the thick door, I bounced on my toes to keep warm, my breath making white fog in the air.

"Hello?"

The door opened a crack, and from what I could tell, a teenager stood peering at me.

"Hi." I smiled, lifting the book in my hand. "I'm Sedona, and I'm looking for Micah Westbrook. He ordered something from my bookstore."

Whatever hesitancy she'd felt evaporated instantly as the door flew open, revealing a cute brunette wearing white fluffy unicorn slippers.

"You brought me my book!" she exclaimed, pulling the package from my arms and hugging it to her chest. "Micah said that he ordered it, but I was afraid it was never, ever, ever going to get here!"

"Holly?" came a deep voice from within the house. "What did I tell you about answering the—" And then he appeared—the man I'd had a hard time forgetting. Not that I wanted to. "—door?"

Much to my mortification, I let out a small gasp as I drank in the sight of him. Wearing dark blue jeans with a regular green flannel shirt, the man was attractive, but that wasn't what elicited such a reaction from me.

It was the glorious yellow shimmer that glowed around his entire body. I'd never seen anything so bright or so beautiful. There was a purity about it that stole my breath.

"Hi, Mr. Westbrook," I stammered, desperately trying to gather my thoughts.

So much for being professional.

"Your book came in early, so I thought I'd drop it by instead of waiting for you to come to the store. From the looks of it, I made the right call." I chuckled lightly and pointed to his niece. "I think I saved her from the torment of waiting forever, and ever, and ever."

"Don't be angry, Micah. She's right. You know how hard it is for me to wait when I want something badly!" Heaven help the poor man, but the puppy dog eyes she gave him were powerful enough to melt even the coldest of hearts. Hell, she wasn't even leveling that gaze my way and I wanted to take her back to Shelf Indulgence and tell her to go crazy.

The glow that had encased him vanished. Whatever wall he kept up between him and the world returned. But I still caught a glimmer of gratitude and, dare I say, interest.

My cheeks heated. I could only wish that someone like him would find someone like me interesting.

"Then it seems I'm in your debt, Miss Mathews. Thank you." He'd come to stand by Holly, placing himself slightly in front of her body as if to shield her from something. I didn't have to understand their relationship or read him to know she was someone he felt incredibly protective of.

Her small hand tugged on his shirtsleeve. "Aren't you forgetting something, Micah?" Holly asked, her smile wide and eyes twinkling. She adored him.

His expression grew confused as he looked at me. "I paid for the book when I placed the order, didn't I?"

I nodded, and before I could reassure him he had, Holly piped in again. "You forgot your manners." Then, pushing gently past her uncle, she stared up at me. "Do you have time for a cup of hot apple cider? It's pretty cold outside, and you look like you're part snowman!"

It was on the tip of my tongue to refuse, not wanting to invade their privacy. I could only begin to imagine the interrogation I'd get from Aunt Millicent once she found out I'd been in Micah's home.

He beat me to the punch, however. "My apologies, Sedona." The sound of my name on his lips sent a shiver through me that had nothing to do with the cool temperature. "Please, come in."

The door swung open wider, and I banged my boots on the side of the step before entering. I instantly went on sensory overload, and my gaze swept across the room, taking everything in. If I expected to uncover all his secrets by inspecting his home and the things he collected, then I'd be sorely disappointed. The living room was functional, holding all the appropriate furniture and décor, but it lacked his personal stamp and style. Holly's was all over the cozy room, from the laptop on the table where some website was currently opened up to the several piles of books scattered over the different surfaces. Just the sight of so many volumes brought a smile to my face.

"Can I say how happy I am to have another bookworm here in town?"

Micah was watching me from the entryway that I assumed led to the kitchen. His stare seemed to press against my aura, like he was trying to figure me out as well. I stared at him openly, showing him I wasn't someone to fear or worry over. Whatever he was looking for, he must've found, because the next moment he ducked out of the room and left Holly and me alone.

"I love books. All kinds of books. I love how they smell and the stories they share." Her words gushed out with an excitement akin to my own whenever I talked about my passion for reading. "One day I'm going to be a writer because words are my life!"

"Then, as one reader to another, you are more than welcome to come to Shelf Indulgence and read to your heart's content."

Her eyes widened to the size of saucers. "Seriously? I can read whatever I want?"

I nodded and drew an X over my chest with my finger. "Cross my heart."

You'd have thought I'd given her the moon when she threw her arms around my neck and squeezed tightly. "Thank you! I need to convince Uncle Micah, but I'm sure I can. He likes to think he's all tough and mean, but he's really a soft marshmallow."

"Are you sure of that?"

Micah's appearance caused Holly to squeak in surprise, her face flushing a mottled shade of red. "You can't say no! If you do, I'll run out of books and die!" And to her credit, she gripped her chest and fell dramatically to the floor, one eye peeking to see if he was watching.

"How could I possibly refuse?" Micah's voice was full of love and humor. He adored his niece just as much as she adored him. "There will be ground rules, though. Like always. Miss Mathews and I will discuss them, and if . . ." Holly sat up, holding her breath as she hung on his words. "If I feel it's okay, then we'll arrange for you to visit."

The young girl bounced on the ground, her smile so big that it brightened the whole room. "You are the *best*!"

"Yeah, yeah," he replied, shaking his head slowly. "I hope you remember that next time I tell you no."

Scooping up the book I'd delivered, Holly rushed over to Micah, threw her arms around his waist, and hugged him hard. "I won't ever argue with you again. I promise. Thank you!" And with that, she blew out of the living room like a whirlwind of adolescent hormones.

That left us alone together.

With him studying me as if I was a puzzle to solve.

"I hope you have good intentions, Sedona," he finally said. He hadn't moved closer and instead folded his arms across his chest, leaning against the doorframe. "I love my niece very much, and there's nothing I won't do to protect her."

An ominous chill swept over me, causing the hairs on my arm to rise.

"I'm not sure who you think I am, but I assure you, I'm no one to worry about." I lifted my hand up. "I'm just a girl who owns a bookstore."

His gaze narrowed. "No offense, but looks can be deceiving. I guess we'll just have to see."

His demeanor and response roused my curiosity. I once again sent out my senses in the hopes of picking up something—anything —from him.

He was still a blank slate.

I pushed again, determined to leave with at least some kind of clue.

"You'll have to try much harder than that, Sedona," he bristled. His stare held such intensity that it was hard not to flinch. This was a man I would never want to cross or anger.

"Than what?" I replied, feigning innocence.

"I know about your gifts, and by now, you should know they don't work on me. I hope that's sufficient for you to stop trying to read me." While his tone wasn't cold or unfriendly, it didn't hold the warmth it had before. I missed it.

Bowing my head, I nodded. "I'm sorry to invade your privacy," I murmured softly. "I guess you could say it's an occupational hazard."

His voice thawed slightly, and his gaze softened. "Not all secrets should be uncovered. Trust me. It's more for your benefit than my own." Then with a focus that felt like it pierced my core, Micah added, "Pass that on to your aunt. I am not her enemy, nor will I bring trouble to the Court or Havenwood Falls. I am simply an uncle trying to raise his niece the best he can."

Words failed me. There was an honesty that rung out—truthfulness that whispered he wasn't lying. It was more than I deserved after being caught using my gifts.

"Okay. Hopefully we can be friends, Micah." I stood from where I was sitting, suddenly needing to be anywhere but here. His presence filled the room—pressing back against my senses. "I need to get back to the store, so I'll take a raincheck on that apple cider, okay?"

He nodded. "Perhaps when I bring Holly into town we could go to one of the coffee shops."

He followed silently behind me as I headed toward the front door, pausing long enough to look over my shoulder, one hand already on the doorknob. "Let Holly know that I hope she enjoys King Henry."

"I will."

We stood there—looking at each other—a thousand unspoken words between us.

Just as I reached the end of the walkway, Micah called out. "Be safe, Sedona. Things aren't always as they seem."

Before I could ask him what he meant, he closed the door.

As snow began falling from the heavy clouds above, I gave his home one last look and started back into town, more confused than ever.

CHAPTER 6

Fridays were my absolute favorite because as soon as it turned three o'clock in the afternoon, Shelf Indulgence would be filled with the sounds of children's excited chatter and giggles. I'd started the tradition of story time the previous year, and it had proven to be a huge success.

Usually it was just me, wearing my special "reading hat" and spectacles, making sure each character had its own distinct voice, much to the merriment of each of my little visitors.

Today's book had reduced us to fits of laughter. *Hugs and Kisses* was a cute story of a little girl catching her parents sharing a sweet kiss and wanting to make sure she knew how to when she grew up. Belle, the confused heroine of the tale, had then gone around her house, kissing her stuffed animals, the mirror, and even her sleeping grandfather's bald head. In her mind, she wanted to be happy just like her mom and dad, and the book ended in a loud symphony of lip smacks—and groans from those who worried about catching cooties from others.

The doorbell sounded, and everyone turned around to see who'd come to join in. I was a little surprised to find Holly standing there, alone, glancing about the store before her gaze met mine.

"Oops," she quickly said, her eyes taking in the small group of children sitting around me. "I don't want to interrupt. I was just hoping to maybe look through some of the shelves . . . like you were talking about earlier with my uncle."

Speaking of Micah, there was no sign of Mr. Tall, Dark, and Broody.

I hoped the smile I gave her helped ease her uncertainty. "Sure. If you find something interesting, there's an oversized chair in the back that is super comfy."

There was a tug at my sleeve. "Miss Sedona, can she read us another story?" Big, round chocolate-brown eyes looked up at me. Even though I told myself I shouldn't have favorites, this little boy knew how to tug hard at my heartstrings.

"I think you need to ask her, sweetheart."

Everyone turned again, watching Holly expectantly.

A huge grin spread across her adolescent features, and she brushed her long, thick brown hair back over her shoulder.

"Of course!" she exclaimed, before coming to join us on the rainbow-colored rug I used for story time.

Not missing a beat, the boy hurried over to the overflowing stack of books I always kept close by. I was pretty sure we'd read through most of them, but it didn't seem to bother anyone. For me, it was about seeing their imaginations expand and blossom. By capturing their hearts now, I hoped they would become forever readers.

"Read this one! It's funny, but you've got to do all the voices. It's only good if you do that." The earnest expression in his gaze had me stifling a chuckle, because I knew he was being as serious as his four-year-old mind could be.

"You sure you don't mind?" Holly asked me. There was no mistaking her excitement. While I didn't know too much about her and Micah, something whispered that she wanted to do this just as much as the children did.

Standing up, I leaned in and quietly added, "Just be careful. If they have their way, they'll have you reading all night."

Of course, when I looked back down at them, each child reflected an image of perfect innocence. The little stinkers!

"Oh, I don't mind. I was getting a little stir crazy anyway." There was no mistaking the sharp twang of loneliness I felt from her. Poor kid was probably bored from constantly staring at the four walls of her home.

Holly took the vacated seat in front of her attentive audience, and I took that as my cue to return to the work I'd left sitting under the register at the front.

Lavender was curled up in her favorite spot by the window, soaking up the warm rays of the sun shining through. I'd discovered the tiny ball of fur late one night, abandoned by the dumpsters outside, shivering with cold. After a brief inspection, I saw that the poor kitten had been born with a deformed, infected leg that made it difficult for her to get about and search for food.

It had taken a few trips to the vet clinic before the doctor deemed it necessary for her to lose the limb. I instantly handed over my credit card, assuring him that Lavender would have a forever home with me and that we were kindred spirits of sorts.

He'd given me a weird look at that, but he was used to it, living in Havenwood Falls. Nothing was ever what it seemed, so why wouldn't a twenty-four-year-old bookstore owner take a disabled kitten into her life? It wouldn't be the strangest thing he'd see in his career.

When I looked into Lavender's eyes, I felt a deep, resounding connection. Both of us knew what it was like to be misunderstood. All we wanted was to be loved for who we were, and not judged solely on our limitations—or in my case, my ability to see into the hearts and minds of those around me.

It was with that peace and calmness that I named the sweet tabby after the purple herb lavender. Had I known her true temperament, I may have chosen Diva instead, or Queen Sassy Pants. But she made me smile, and her early morning meowing for food was more endearing than annoying.

Most days.

"Enjoying the view, Lavender?" I asked, gently brushing my fingers over her soft fur. "See anything interesting happening out there?"

I peered out the bay windows, wishing for the time when the town square would return to its gorgeous manicured green lawns and gardens.

They'd finally taken down the Valentine's Day decorations in preparation for the upcoming spring equinox celebrations. There was always something happening—some party, fair, or festival.

I especially liked the Into the Mystic New Age & Psychic Fair Eloise planned each year that ran during the equinox. It was one of those occasions where some of the supernaturals in town could be themselves, sharing their gifts and talents with the unsuspecting, yet enthusiastic, human population. Eloise had tried to convince me to buy a booth and use my empath skills with some kind of love theme. So far I'd managed to sidestep her insistent asking. It seemed a sham to help others find love when I couldn't do it for myself.

Lavender purred beneath my touch, her fur rippling as she leisurely stretched.

Austin came rushing through the door, sending a cold draft of air in and ruffling the flyers on the counter. I didn't know who was more annoyed—me or my pampered cat. She threw him a disdainful look before closing her eyes again.

"Sorry I'm late. I ran all the way from school." Dumping his heavy backpack behind the counter, he kissed my cheek, grabbing his name badge at the same time. "I was beginning to think I was going to die in that last period. Why the hell did I take AP Statistics again?"

I rolled my eyes at him. "Because, and I quote, what's life for except to live a little dangerously." I lowered my hands after making quotation marks in the air. "I believe you also mentioned that it would be fun."

I still had a hard time accepting my part-time employee took hard subjects like math because he thought it would be fun. The only entertaining thing about that would be watching how many brains exploded from mental calculations and test anxiety. My own time in school was purposely blocked out, so I never remembered the trauma of trying to memorize equations and formulas.

Words I loved.

The alphabet had no business in math.

"Well, I'm seriously rethinking that theory and questioning how reliable my common sense is. Why didn't I take some fluff class like pottery making or papier mâché? I could've graduated *and* made a cool Christmas present for my annoying cousin, Ling." Austin smoothed down his wind-blown hair and glanced around. "So, who's the new girl?"

There was a glint of interest in his eyes and a ping in his aura.

"She's fourteen," I answered, sharply. Austin was a good kid, but he was also a flirt. The last thing I wanted was Micah storming in because his niece was suffering from a broken heart. "So go easy on the poor girl. Not everyone is immune to your charm."

His boyish grin made it hard to remain stern. He really did have a good heart, from what I could tell. He did what he wanted. He wore what he wanted. There wasn't much he couldn't talk himself out of or into. That was how he came to work for me. He wanted a part-time job and had decided Shelf Indulgence was in dire need of his services. After five minutes of listening to him, I was shoving the new-hire paperwork at him.

Austin placed his hand over his chest while feigning shock and offense. "You wound me, Sedona. You truly do. I was simply asking who she was. No other motives. Pinky swear."

I rolled my eyes at him again. "Just get to work and leave her alone. Go through the books and make sure everything's in order and where it should be."

He bowed dramatically, rolling his hand out in front of him. "As you wish."

And just because he could, he took a slight detour by the small group of attentive listeners and winked at Holly. She forgot her place in the story for the briefest of seconds, but it was enough to earn a response from the children. Stammering, she returned her focus to the book and continued on.

I wanted to throttle Austin.

"I'll gladly do it for you, Sedona. He won't feel it, but I would take great pleasure in the mere action of it."

My life was utterly crazy, with a diva cat, a Casanova employee, and a ghost who never gave a warning when he popped in and out from wherever he went when he wasn't bothering me.

"You know, it's not healthy to keep all that suppressed anger bottled up, Maxwell. You should learn to relax." I gave him a sidelong glance before reaching under the counter for the small pile of order forms and bills. "Maybe you should channel your inner Casper."

The snort of indignation that erupted from him made my teasing worth it. "You would mourn me if I ever decided to leave this establishment. Don't try to deny it."

"Not if you keep threatening to inflict ghostly bodily harm on Austin. How many times is it this week? Eight? Ten?" I'd lost count.

"Twelve, but that's beside the point. You refuse to listen to me when I warn you something isn't quite right about him. Mark my words, you'll regret not listening to me, Sedona."

Austin could never see Maxwell when they were both in the same room, but sometimes I wondered if he really could. Now was one of those moments because, as if hearing his name, Austin looked back toward the front at me.

I refused to give any credence to Maxwell's paranoia. Austin was as hardworking as he was smart, and he had a sense of style that I admired. Today, he wore a pair of blue denim jeans with a red-and-yellow-striped T-shirt that had a Gryffindor patch on the breast. He loved to dress up for the different events in the community, wearing his fandom favorites with pride.

"He's harmless," I countered, repeating the same thing I did each time the topic came up. "Don't you think I'd sense if something was off about him?" I glared at him, tired of having to defend Austin. "Seriously. I think I'm a pretty good judge of character." I tried not to be offended when he cocked his eyebrows at me and scoffed. I continued, "Fine, besides some of the guys I've dated."

"You're still very young, Sedona, as are your gifts. And because of your youth and naiveté, you often ignore what's right before you."

"Well, right now, I have a grumpy old man standing in front of me. How's that for talent?" I hated arguing with Maxwell. I knew he had good intentions, but he wasn't my father. He didn't have a right to tell me how to live my life.

He instantly closed his mouth, pursing his lips. The edges around his form began to grow hazy. He was about to fade away. I didn't stop him this time. We would no doubt talk later, and all would be forgiven.

I guess he wasn't done lecturing me. Just as he was almost gone, I heard him say, "Mark my words, Sedona. Mark. My. Words."

I plopped back onto the counter stool and stared at the empty space where he had just been. Our conversation had left a weird taste in my mouth, and I felt myself nearing my limit. Being an empath could be exhausting, and there were days when I found myself suddenly overstimulated and in desperate need of solitude.

The clock on the wall behind me said it was already four. Parents would be coming for their children soon, and maybe I could close up early for the day. The safety of my home felt very appealing right now.

"What say you, Lavender? Shall we go home and spend the night watching *Kitchen Nightmares* on Hulu?"

She ignored me.

I guess it would just be me then.

Sorting through the papers, I took care of the most urgent and important, then placed the pile back under the counter for tomorrow. I was starting to get a headache, and the numbers on the bills had begun swimming on the page.

With my head resting in my hands, my eyes closed. I didn't see him coming until he was standing in the entryway, fists clenched, thunder echoing in his voice as he glared at me.

"Where is she?" Micah demanded, his anger filling the store until there was no room to even breathe. He was magnificent as much as he was terrifying.

Two of the children began to cry.

"Micah," I started, instantly choking as he advanced toward me.

It was then that I felt it—fear . . . panic . . . uncertainty.

It was in total contradiction to the body language he was displaying.

Micah Westbrook was terrified, and he looked like he would level the town in his wrath.

I tried again, gulping nervously before finding the courage to face him.

"She's here, Micah." That was when I realized she hadn't told him where she was going. She'd been here all this time, and I'd foolishly assumed he'd known.

It took a few moments for him to register what I said, and a few more for him to notice that Holly had come to stand beside him, her hand lying gently on his bicep.

"Uncle."

And in the space it took for him to finally see her and take a breath, his emotions were locked back behind the wall he always had erected. But I'd been prepared this time—quicker. I'd caught some images that had flashed in his mind before it all went blank.

He looked at me, knowing I'd seen something with my gift.

Wrapping his arms around Holly, he crushed her to him, all the while telling her to never, ever leave the house again without telling him. His eyes never left mine, even though he was talking to his niece. Part of me wanted to feign interest in my paperwork so they could have a little privacy, but I wasn't the only one watching the encounter.

"Perhaps you two would like to use the back storeroom to talk?" I suggested.

"No, we're leaving. Grab your things, Holly." There was a heavy dose of authority in his tone that most people would struggle to ignore. It demanded obedience and submission. It wouldn't tolerate defiance, which was exactly what Holly showed.

With her hands firmly on her waist, she glared up at her uncle. "I'm not ready to leave yet. I haven't finished reading the story. Plus, you're angry."

I could almost hear Micah count to ten in his mind. I wanted to laugh and remind him that it only got worse with teenagers—that if he thought he could win every battle with her, he was sadly deluded.

"Fine, let's talk." Gesturing for her to go ahead, he looked my way again. "The room is back there?"

"Yes," I nodded. "Take your time."

The storefront was eerily quiet once the two had left and the door closed swiftly behind them. The children shifted uneasily, and I threw on another smile just for them.

"How about we have another story while we wait for your parents?"

It was the longest ten minutes I'd ever spent in the store as I attempted to read, watching nervously where Micah and Holly had disappeared, and also the front door. Finally the last of the children were gone.

Austin snuck up beside me. "What the heck was that?" he murmured, letting out a low whistle.

"Good question," I answered.

Unfortunately, I didn't have a clue either.

CHAPTER 7

*I*t was difficult not to say anything as Micah and Holly walked past me on their way out of the store. Some of the intensity that had been rolling off Micah had subsided, and poor Holly meekly followed behind him.

She quickly apologized for any problems her coming had created, and before I could reassure her that she was more than welcome to visit, Micah tugged on her hand, and they were gone.

I closed up Shelf Indulgence shortly after that, exhausted. The whole afternoon had been one hell of an emotional roller coaster, and all I wanted was to hide away in my fortress of an apartment with Lavender and forget the world existed.

"I wonder what Gordon's up to tonight, Lavender?" I asked as I clicked on the television, scrolling through my DVR for the episodes of *Hell's Kitchen* I'd saved. Slowly stroking her soft fur, I smiled as her loud purrs filled the room. "What do you think my chances are of meeting him?" Relaxing back into the couch, I curled my feet up beneath me. "A girl can dream, right?"

Gradually, all the events of the day melted away, and I finally found my happy place. The specialty peppermint tea I'd purchased from Broastful Brew left a soothing path down my throat, and everything was perfect and in order.

Chaos often spelled disaster for an empath, because it was the quickest way to overstimulate the senses and send them spiraling into overload. It was why I made sure I was always protected with the charmed pendant I'd fashioned out of black tourmaline. It helped keep any negative energy out of my aura and prevented it from seeping into my own consciousness. Today I'd been caught off guard.

"Okay, my darling." The sexy British accent on the television pulled me back to the present, and I smiled. Goose bumps spread across my bare arms. If only I had someone to speak such endearments to me.

"I need to get a life, Lavender," I murmured, looking around my small apartment.

I'd been living at Havenwood Village for the past three years and spent most of it decorating my one-bedroom home with things that usually filled me with a calm sense of satisfaction. Tonight, however, it was merely a reminder of how alone I truly was—a loneliness I often hid from myself.

The spoiled cat opened one eye, as if to say she agreed, before shutting it again.

Suddenly, I didn't want to be hidden away in my apartment. I was tired of spending yet another night watching pre-recorded shows before trudging off to bed. I wanted to be where everyone else was—experiencing life in all its glory. It was time to shake off the introvert and embrace the part of me that loved being social.

I quickly slipped into jeans, a pretty top, and flats, then grabbed my keys and bag.

"Don't wait up, Lavender! I have no idea how long I'll be or when I'll be home." Throwing open the door with a huge grin on my face, my impromptu adventure was pulled to an abrupt stop.

Micah Westbrook stood on the other side, his hand poised as if he was about to knock. I didn't know who was more surprised—me or him.

Damn, he smells amazing!

He cleared his throat, looking unsure as he glanced over his shoulder to where he'd come from.

"Did I catch you at a bad time?" There was a sexy rasp in his voice that I hadn't noticed before. It skimmed over my senses, leaving a trail of tingles in its wake.

I looked down at my hand to my keys. "I . . . well, I was . . ." *Damn, I sound like an idiot.* "I was thinking about going to the Haven Saloon."

Micah's eyes narrowed as he studied me. "I've never seen you there before."

My face heated, and I wanted to curse whoever's genes gave me this inclination to blush all the time. I was a grown woman, and yet, the way Micah's gaze bored into me, I wanted to confess all my secrets.

"Would you like to join me?" I blurted out.

A slow smile crawled across his handsome features. "Will you be meeting someone there?"

My stomach did a flip as I confessed that I was planning to go by myself.

"Then I'd be happy to escort you there."

Locking the door behind me, I walked silently beside him as we made our way down to the street. How had this happened? What made me think I even stood a chance with a man like him? He was so confident, while I preferred the company of books and animals. He held all the mystique of a newcomer, while I was someone people often kept their distance from because I might sense some dark and foreboding truth.

When he took my hand and placed it in the crook of his arm, I threw caution to the wind. I relaxed. I let out a breath. I released the anxiety knitting a knot in my stomach.

I'd said I needed to get a life, and the Fates had answered.

The question was . . . what kind of life had I just agreed to?

"DID you know that the tune of 'The Star-Spangled Banner' was borrowed from the melody of an old drinking song?"

Micah cocked his brow in interest. "Really?"

I could understand why he was skeptical. It was such a patriotic song, beloved by everyone.

"Yep," I answered. "The original was the song of a British gentlemen's music club some two hundred years ago." I took a small sip of the beer I'd ordered. I had no clue why I'd chosen it, but after a few mouthfuls, the hoppy taste didn't bother me as much.

Micah rested his head on his hand, the fingers of his other hand lightly curled around his own glass. "You're a wealth of information, Miss Mathews. What other tidbits do you know?"

I didn't know whether he was genuinely curious or teasing me, but I didn't care. The beer was warm in my body, and my energy was thrumming from all the people surrounding us. The saloon was busy tonight, and we almost didn't find a table. Fortunately for us, there were a few in the very back, and we'd rushed forward to claim one of them.

I raised my glass, tilting it slightly to the side as the amber liquid sloshed back and forth.

"Did you know that the world's oldest known recipe is for beer? Or that it's illegal to feed alcohol to moose in Alaska and fishes in Ohio?" When he went to respond, I took a quick sip before continuing, "Or that there is a cloud of alcohol in outer space that holds enough booze to make trillions of drinks?"

"You're making that last one up!" Micah exclaimed, incredulously.

"Nope, it's all true. Just one of many useful facts I have stored up here." I tapped the side of my head, grinning. "Or useless. I haven't quite decided on that yet."

He leaned forward on his elbows, close enough for me to catch another whiff of his spicy cologne. I absently licked my lips as my gaze dropped to his chest. I was a freaking lightweight when it came to alcohol. Half a glass, and I was contemplating what facts could convince him to take his shirt off.

"Why do you do that?"

It was my turn to wear a quizzical look. "Do what?"

His nails tapped gently against the surface of his glass. "Whenever you're nervous, you become a fount of knowledge. You did the same that first time we met."

I shrugged. "I don't know. I guess I find a certain comfort in facts . . . in truths. People often confuse me, especially when I can't figure out their intentions. It's why I love reading and books. The only surprises are the plot twists the author throws in."

The air seemed to still around us, dimming the music that played in the bar. "Do I confuse you, Sedona?"

I was tempted to lie and fake bravado, but I knew he'd see right through it. Micah was good at reading people . . . he'd known straight away about my gifts, and that I was trying to use them on him.

"Truthfully?" I held his gaze as he nodded.

"Naturally."

A small blast of heat went through me. "You don't confuse me as much as scare me a little."

He hadn't looked away. "How so?"

Licking my lips, I sat up a little straighter. "Well, for starters, I can't get a lock on your emotions. The only people I can't read are those who purposely shield themselves from me. As far as I know, you don't really know me, so why would you hide?"

His eyes were like the crystal blue waters of the Bahamas. "And is that what you want? To have me lower my guard and let you in?"

If I were to guess what kind of supernatural he was, I would say he was a warlock, because he'd somehow created this web of attraction between us.

"What are you hiding from me?" I countered, my voice low.

"We all have secrets, Sedona. It isn't always good to be so open with everyone."

There he was again with his cryptic talking. "But isn't that part of becoming friends with people? Of developing relationships? It's about give and take. It's about letting someone in and showing them pieces of yourself."

"Is that what you want from me? To be friends?"

"Don't you?" I fired back. "I may not know you too well, but I know another lonely soul when I meet one. You're extremely guarded. The only time I've felt any semblance of emotion from you is with Holly." Instantly, the shutters fell in his eyes, and I let him know I saw it. "See? I mention Holly, and suddenly you clam up tighter than a bank vault. I know you said to be careful with who you trust, but isn't life too short to keep everyone at arm's length?"

I let my question hang in the air between us. Resting back in my chair, I cradled the glass in front of me between my hands. "All I'm saying is it's okay to trust someone, Micah. It's okay to let people in. We're not all villains or whoever you seem to think we are."

He sat quietly, his lips closed as he mulled over my passionate rambling. As the seconds ticked slowly by, panic began to fill me. This was why I shouldn't ever go out in public. I wasn't good with people, and sometimes—well, often—I shoved both feet in my mouth.

I started feeling desperate, so I did what I always did in such occasions.

"Did you know chewing gum while peeling onions can keep you from crying?"

He remained still until he burst out laughing. It defused the tension, and I joined in.

Once he eventually stopped, Micah nodded. "I think I'd like to be your friend, too, Sedona. Perhaps you are someone I can trust."

"While I can't promise you I won't bore you with more facts, I can promise you that you won't regret it." Raising my glass in the air, I clinked it against his. "To being friends."

His voice was thick as he murmured the same.

I placed the glass back on the table, glad to have that all out of the way. "So, you never did tell me why you came over tonight."

His eyes widened when he realized the same. "I simply wanted to apologize for my poor behavior today at your store. I let my fear for Holly get the best of me when I couldn't find her. We talked about it, so knock on wood." He rapped his knuckles on the tabletop. "You won't ever see me acting like a raving lunatic again."

There it was again—that niggling thread that just begged for me to tug on. "You're a good uncle to worry about your niece. Havenwood Falls is pretty safe, though. Maybe you don't have to worry *as* much now."

His mouth twitched as he shook his head. "I'll always worry, but that's a story for another time. For the time being, she can continue coming to the store on the condition that she call me once she gets there."

"You're really protective of her, aren't you?" I said, hoping it would lead to him sharing why. There was no such luck, however. When he said it was a tale for another day, he meant it.

Giving him a sly look as I finished my drink, I warned Micah that sooner or later I would figure him out.

"Be careful what you wish for, Sedona. That's all I'm going to say. Be careful."

If only someone could tell that to my heart.

CHAPTER 8

*A*pparently what Micah had meant that night at the Haven Saloon was that he would watch Holly like a hawk regardless of whether she called him.

I still didn't know what hidden dangers lurked inside his head, and trust me, it irked me to no end that I couldn't seem to penetrate the wall he had around his mind, but it didn't take a rocket scientist to see why he suddenly became a fixture at Shelf Indulgence.

Just one word: Austin.

Holly had spent just one afternoon with my employee, and it was plain to see that she was well on her way to a full-blown case of teenage angst and puppy love. Whether Austin realized it or not, I noticed the longing stares she cast his way and how she twisted a strand of her hair between her fingers. But those signs paled in comparison to the rather large flashing neon sign that seemed to hang above her that screamed CRUSH.

I took care not to invade her emotions, knowing just how hard it was at that age, when you first discovered boys and that they were more than just cootie carriers. It had been tempting to pry a little and see if I could uncover Micah's secrets through her. I hated the sleazy feeling that skated over my senses as part of me warred with the other.

No one would know if I did decide to push just a little bit against Holly's defenses. Well, someone would know—me.

Besides, the more time I spent with the kid, the more I grew to like her. Her thirst for knowledge was refreshing, and it was satisfying watching her voraciously devouring each book she pulled from the shelf.

Then Austin sauntered through the door in all his shiny senior glory, and Holly found a new subject to enjoy. I had a quick word with Austin to remind him that she was off limits and that if I caught him leading her on, I would put him on toilet duty for a year. He scoffed at my attempt at a threat, replying that one toilet wasn't that big of a deal, considering he already took care of it. His face blanched a sickly shade of white, however, when I told him I hadn't quite finished. I would see that he cleaned every toilet on town square and the surrounding businesses, and that if he didn't believe me, I'd throw in the ski resort for good measure.

I didn't really have that kind of pull, but it was funny to watch the belief in his eyes. Austin was then on his best behavior and volunteered to tutor Holly with her schoolwork. She impressed him immediately with her knowledge, and they spent most afternoons with their heads down as they read from some textbook or another.

Harmless enough to me.

Worrisome to Micah.

"I don't like him," he murmured, not once taking his eyes off the pair. "Are you sure you threatened him enough? Perhaps I should have a talk with him."

I studied Micah as he stood leaning against the wall that led to the back storeroom. I was once again perched on my stool behind the counter, scrolling through a list of books I was hoping to order from. I clicked out of that window and opened another, this one the site where I often purchased the decorations for my window display. I'd finally narrowed the list down to a spring theme, considering the spring equinox was fast approaching.

Who was I kidding? I'd spent more time memorizing the leanness of his body and how his jaw tightened each time Austin moved closer to Holly. He was watching them, and I was watching him. My heart raced faster whenever he looked my way, and it became increasingly harder to focus. Suddenly I understood Holly a little better—we both had crushes on guys way out of our league.

"Are you seriously going to stand there ready to pounce on that poor boy?" I asked, laughing. "What do you think he's going to do? Whisk her away to Mexico and get married? Get her drunk at some frat party?"

I was only teasing, but for a second there, I worried the muscle in Micah's tight jaw might snap from pressure. His glare was positively lethal.

"He'll be dead before he takes his next breath," he muttered softly below his breath, poised to take a step toward the two unaware teens.

"Micah!" I exclaimed, my eyes widening. A sick sensation settled in the pit of my stomach, and a menacing, oppressive wave flowed over me. He wasn't joking around. Deep in my gut I knew that what he had spoken out loud was truth.

Moving away from where I was sitting, I cautiously approached him, trying to figure out what had flipped the anger switch inside him. Yes, most males got overly protective when members of the opposite sex so much as breathed too close to their female family members, but this was excessive.

I had to think quickly and defuse the situation. Catching him off guard, I shoved hard at him, pushing him back into the storage room, and slammed the door closed with my foot. I was getting ready to lay the law down with him.

"I may look small, Micah Westbrook, but believe me when I tell you that I won't hesitate to knock you on your ass if you don't start acting with better manners. I've known that kid out there for a year, so you can trust me when I say he's a good kid."

Micah began to speak, but I cut him off.

"I'm not finished." I jabbed at his chest with my finger, which earned me a soft grunt. The corners of his mouth trembled as he tried not to smile.

Great. He thought I was being cute.

"You've got two choices, mister. You can either leave, and I'll call you when their tutoring session is over, or you can quit acting like a caveman and be useful."

He cocked his eyebrow, intrigued. "Useful how?"

"Well, for starters you can stop acting like a helicopter parent, hovering in anticipation, and help me organize in here." I gestured to my neatly arranged shelves of inventory. "And before you make some sarcastic remark, this system no longer works for me." My hands rested on my hips as I stared him down.

"Are those the only two options I have?" For some reason, his gaze dropped to my mouth before rising again to meet my stare.

"Well," I began, wearing a smirk of my own. "You can always choose door number three and explain to me why you want to kill anyone who gets close to Holly. You know that's not normal, right? Keep acting this way, and I'm going to start thinking your secret is you're a serial killer on the run."

He had the audacity to bark out a loud laugh, tears forming at the corner of his eyes. "Is that what you think, Sedona?"

He took a step toward me, blocking the way out with his body.

I stood my ground, not intimidated in the least. "I don't know what to think, Micah. You refuse to answer any of my questions, remember?"

I tilted my head back slightly so I could still hold eye contact. Good lord, he was tall. I briefly closed my eyes. I could still feel him. *Damn it.*

"What if I told you I'm feeling generous today?" He stepped even closer, and the room suddenly felt too small, my own emotions bouncing off the walls. Instinctively, I searched for his, and once again felt the tall, hard wall he'd erected as a defense.

No, wait.

Somewhere in the few moments that had passed, my traitorous hand had reached out and now rested over his heart. The hardness that I felt was in fact . . . him.

"Sedona," he murmured, his tone now soft and gentle. I wanted to lean into him. "Tell me what you want."

A thousand responses raced through my mind—from all the questions I had to the private fantasies I entertained late at night while I was safe at home.

He tilted my chin up with his finger. The look on his face melted me because it brought a different emotion for him into the forefront, one I hadn't expected.

Desire.

"Micah," I breathed, licking my lips. "Just let me in. Trust me." I was about to add *and don't kill my employee*, when he surprised me again.

"Okay." It was just one word, but I knew how much it meant for him to grant it. "Feel this."

I gasped out loud as I felt his walls come down, and the sweetest, most intense sensation spilled out from behind it.

Attraction.

Desire.

Interest.

A wild desperation at having to deny the one thing he wanted—me.

One word filled my mind that confused me.

Forbidden.

I parted my lips to ask him why he saw me that way, but he didn't give me a chance, because he crushed his mouth over mine, his tongue tracing the seam of my lips. My arms wrapped around his neck, and his hands spanned my waist, bringing my body up against his. I didn't know whether it was because I was up on my tiptoes or because he'd lifted me up off the ground, but we fit perfectly. His kiss was beyond perfect. In fact, it far exceeded anything I could've hoped for.

In that one kiss I knew he had ruined me for any that may follow. He savored each taste, each dip of his tongue as it met with mine, causing both of us to moan softly. It was both beautiful and savage—beautiful because he held me like I was precious and savage because there was a barely restrained hunger that lurked beneath the kiss.

I wanted to encourage him to let go of whatever kept him always on guard.

I wanted to tell him—scream—that it was okay and that nothing catastrophic would happen—that we were both consenting adults who wanted this. I felt myself melt in his arms and his embrace tighten, holding me closer. It was everything and more, and I begged that time could stand still so I could memorize every blissful second.

His hand skated up over my back and into my hair, his fingers curling in the strands. A thought flashed through my mind to never wear it down again because electricity sizzled through my nerves, setting them on fire.

I felt alive—painfully, blissfully aware of everything around me.

And then the moment was over, and I could feel him pull back. I kept my eyes closed as if to prolong the numbness of my lips, the touch of his hands on my body.

"Sedona," he whispered, his voice low and husky.

"Mmmm," I replied, and I slowly opened my eyes.

"Did you know King Henry the Sixth banned kissing in England as a way to prevent the spread of disease? Or that the average person spends two weeks of their life kissing?"

My eyes flew open as I burst out laughing. "Oh, really?"

His grin showed me more than tapping into his emotions would. He was very proud of himself. "I also read that scientists at the University in Tokyo believe our love of kissing comes from an ancient rat."

My brow furrowed, and I scrunched my nose. "Ewwww, I'm almost too scared to ask about that last one, but I have to know!"

I locked eyes with him again, enjoying his impromptu fact sharing.

"Yeah, I wasn't quite sure I wanted to share that with you, but I also knew your thirst for knowledge—the weirder the better." He brushed the hair away from the side of my face, his fingers slowly trailing down before cupping my cheek. "I'm hoping it will earn me brownie points in case that kiss was an epic fail."

My mouth watered, and I wanted to grab his face to kiss him back. Hard. "I never pegged you for someone who lacked confidence in that area, Micah," I teased. "But yes, you earned big points for those pieces of trivia. In fact, I have it on good authority that if you tell me more about that ancient rat, there will be another kiss." I sounded cheesy as hell, but I didn't care.

"Something about the rat rubbing noses with its mate to signal desire." Micah leaned in, placing his forehead against mine, our noses barely touching. "I didn't expect to find you, Sedona." His warm breath fanned across my lips.

"Yet here we are."

He leaned in again, whispering against my mouth, "I guess this changes everything."

And with that declaration, my heart soared.

CHAPTER 9

There was no denying the extra little bounce in my step or the huge smile plastered across my face was because of Micah. I was turning into one of the heroines in my beloved books who can finally claim the man they love.

Not that I loved Micah, but hell, I was definitely falling.

There was something about him that instantly drew my gaze whenever he was in the room—his presence filled the entire space. He took my breath away with the simplest things, those small considerations that showed he was paying attention.

If I thought he was protective of Holly, that awareness had now spread to cover me. In the weeks since our first kiss, I often wondered what had rattled him so badly and set his instincts on fire. He was always vigilant when we were together, even when I shared a meal with him and Holly in their home. Every noise caused him to pause momentarily, as if he was waiting for something to crash in and attack.

It was torturous not to blurt out my questions whenever he got that faraway look in his eye, a sign that he was thinking . . . listening. I fought the temptation to casually ask Holly if she understood her uncle's driving need to protect, but I knew in my heart that was crossing a line. It was something my aunt would do—something she encouraged me to use my gift for.

"Why would you be given such an important gift, dear niece, unless you were expected to serve the coven? Don't you want to help keep Havenwood Falls safe and free from nefarious creatures?"

It didn't matter how many times I argued that it went against my ethics. I was a tool to be used, plain and simple.

It was because of Aunt Millicent that I reined in my curiosity when it came to Micah. I wouldn't stoop to her level. I wouldn't prove her right when she said that one day I would regret not listening to her.

"You'll call me when you're done, right?" Micah asked as he lifted my hand to his mouth and kissed it. He'd insisted on walking me to my hair appointment at Shear Magic. His expression was kind of cute when I casually wondered out loud who he thought would attack me as I walked the short distance from the bookstore. He tutted beneath his breath and gripped my hand a little tighter.

"It might be late," I replied, bouncing slowly on the balls of my feet, looking up at him. "It's usually an all-day thing when I change hair color."

Micah twisted a strand of my hair around his finger. "Explain to me again why you're doing this? You're beautiful, sweetheart, and wouldn't it make you stand out?"

I nodded at the last of his response. I did want to stand out. I was finally ready to step back out into the world and participate. Maybe it was Micah who gave me this newfound sense of courage, because with him, I didn't feel so scared.

"I had to cancel my last appointment because I was sick, and this was the first opportunity I could get back in. Besides," I grinned playfully, "it's not every day a girl can get hair like a mermaid."

"And that's a good thing?" His quizzical expression was adorable.

"It's a very good thing." Rising back onto my tiptoes again, I pressed my mouth against his firmly. A sense of brief frustration flittered across my senses—his. "I promise you'll like it."

"Perhaps I should stay," he murmured, lips pursed.

"Are you imagining a fleet of ninjas rappelling from the salon's ceiling? Perhaps karate-chopping us into submission?" I gently teased him even though I knew his concerns were real to him. "Seriously, go glare at Austin for a few hours. He mentioned Holly coming in to work on some homework. You know how young men can be."

It was a mean thing to say, but Micah responded exactly how I thought he would. One mention of Holly, and all thoughts of my being assaulted while getting my hair colored were shoved onto the back burner.

I knew where I ranked compared to his niece, and it didn't bother me in the slightest.

He kissed me once more, chuckling under his breath when we pulled apart. Glancing over my shoulder, I caught the gaze of one of the ladies inside the salon.

"Looks like we have an audience, Micah." I couldn't hide my amusement. I didn't try to as I openly laughed.

He quickly hooked his arm back around my waist and tugged me up close.

"Then let's give them something to talk about."

And what a kiss it was.

I WAS AFFORDED at least an hour before I heard his name mentioned. After entering Shear Magic, I'd made a beeline to the stack of magazines, randomly choosing one as I buried my nose in the thrilling gossip of some celebrity and their inner turmoil. I feigned complete interest, avoiding eye contact with anyone until finally my own name was called.

"We still doing the mermaid look, Sedona?" Charlotte asked, peering at my reflection in the mirror I now sat before. Charlie, for short, was a genius when it came to hair, and the only person in Havenwood Falls I would trust with mine. She'd squealed with excitement when I showed her a photo I'd found online and vowed she wouldn't let me leave the salon until my hair was perfect.

I didn't know too much about Charlie other than the basics. Like me, she kept pretty much to herself unless it had something to do with work. I got the impression that life hadn't been easy for her and knew should she choose to open up, she would. Today she had her fiery red hair pinned back with a set of fashion chopsticks stuck expertly into her loose bun. Tendrils of hair framed her round face, and a warm smile graced her features. Every time I came in, I made a mental note to somehow get to know her better, but life often got in the way.

"Absolutely!" I grinned as I tucked my feet on the chair's rung. "I can't tell you how many times I've seen that photo. The purples, blues, and greens are gorgeous!"

She whipped the black plastic cape around me and began running her fingers through my hair. "Did you want a trim after to keep it healthy?" She held up a section, showing me the length she intended to cut. "Probably about half an inch would do it."

Closing my eyes, I relaxed into the swivel seat. "I'm in your capable hands, Charlie. I trust you."

A while later, I sat with my head under a dryer, the foil hiding the different dyes within its folds, making me look like I was trying to ward off a legion of space aliens. I'd started off reading another magazine, but it didn't take long before my mind wandered to more enjoyable thoughts.

Like Micah.

His kisses.

The way his eyes widened ever so slightly—giving away how he truly felt whenever he saw me.

How amazing he was with Holly, even when he was being super protective.

He had so many incredibly sexy traits that dazzled me. He made the dashing heroes in my books pale by comparison. I was less interested in reading the pile of romance novels by my bedside and more into experiencing my very own real-life fairy tale.

Part of me warned that I was bordering on delusional—that there was no such thing as the perfect guy. Sooner or later, things would sour, and Micah would walk away. If it was too good to be true, it usually meant that some kind of flaw would surface and tarnish the sparkle.

I didn't want the tarnish.

As silly as it sounded, living where I did, surrounded by supernaturals, I wanted the magic.

"Sedona, dear, perhaps you could settle an argument."

Peering over the top of the magazine I was pretending to read, I found myself the center of attention. Irene Beckett and two other town members, Laverne and Sybil Carson, huddled closer, their hair set in curlers. The way Irene wet her lips with anticipation and her eyes twinkled told me all I needed to know.

Micah. They had caught our kiss goodbye and had been gracious enough to lull me into a false sense of security before pouncing. It almost felt like I was their trapped prey, caught in their web until they gained the answers they were seeking and set me free.

I visibly gulped and faked a smile. Hoping against hope, I feigned ignorance. I wouldn't be making this easy for them.

"Hi, ladies. The salon seems the place to be this morning." I was tempted to lift the magazine back off my lap. I glanced at the clock. I still had another fifteen minutes under the heated dryer.

Sybil leaned in and stared at my foiled head. "Did I see right? You're having your hair colored blue?"

The three human women must've been in their seventies, and I couldn't tell whether they approved or not.

It didn't matter. "Yep, plus purple and green. I call it the mermaid look."

Sybil scrunched up her nose. "It should be interesting," she muttered, her gaze never leaving my covered hair.

That was pretty tame for Mrs. Carson, because she usually had no qualms letting you know exactly how she felt. The three of them shared that same trait. When they all zeroed in their focus on you— heaven help you and God bless. There was a rumor circulating town that they could be so sharp-tongued, their words could flay flesh off bone. An exaggeration, maybe, but the imagery made me shudder.

Her almost kind response further warned me they had another agenda. They had questions, and I was the one who could satisfy their thirst for gossip.

"Miss Mathews," Irene chirped, a sugary smile twisting her lips into an insincere grimace. "Did I see right earlier? Are you and Micah Westbrook an item?"

Before I could answer, Laverne interjected. "I should hope so. Sedona isn't the kind of girl for such grand displays of affection in public. Micah is definitely her beau." She nodded as if it was a commonly known fact and therefore didn't require me to respond.

"You shouldn't be that open with members of the opposite sex, Sedona, dear," Sybil countered, her eyes tinged with concern and her voice low. "You wouldn't want others to think you're something you're not."

I stifled a chuckle. "Thank you for worrying about me, Mrs. Carson, but I'm okay. Yes, Micah and I have started to date."

The three of them collectively took in a deep breath. It made me want to take a bazillion steps back. They reminded me of a nest of cobras, drawing back before they struck.

"About Micah . . ." It was Irene who finally revealed the true reason they surrounded me.

"Mm-hmm," I murmured, praying they'd think better of prying. No such luck.

Irene continued. "Has he told you much about himself? Like who he is or where he came from?"

"Or why he doesn't allow his sweet niece to go to the public school? Why would he prefer to homeschool when we have a fine educational institution at his disposal? Havenwood Falls High is one of the best in the country," Laverne bragged, her chest puffing out with pride.

"I don't really think I should be talking about this without him here." If there was one thing I'd learned, it was the need to be diplomatic. "I'm sure if you asked him, he'd be happy to answer your questions."

It was a bald-faced lie but I didn't care. There was a small voice inside that wanted to add that I couldn't share what I didn't know. My knowledge about Micah was limited as it was. The few tidbits I'd managed to glean were pitiful.

Sybil bounced a little with excitement, and her voice grew louder. "I heard he's part of the witness protection program, and that's why he's here. That he witnessed something so horrifying, he needed to go into hiding."

Her gaze darted back and forth conspiratorially.

"Sedona, are you all right?" Laverne's tone lost its previous nosiness, and motherly concern replaced it. She reached out and touched my hand. "Did we say something wrong?"

Irene zeroed in on me, and I could feel her gaze hungrily search my face for hidden clues. Heaven help everyone if this woman had been gifted with being an empath. She'd gorge herself on all the secrets she'd uncover, because there was no way she would maintain respectful boundaries.

Their stares felt heavy. I shook my head. "I'm fine, and to answer your questions, again, maybe you can ask Micah. He's the best one to share his story."

Something in my voice must've convinced them they were barking up the wrong tree and to back off. They whispered amongst themselves quietly before offering me those sugary smiles again.

"We're glad to see you happy. We just wanted to make sure he was worthy of you."

"Yes, yes," Sybil added, casting a sidelong glance of agreement at Laverne. "Only the best for our beautiful Sedona."

My face heated at the compliment. The way they seemed to bounce back and forth between pushing for gossip and buttering me up with praise gave me a headache.

"Sedona," Charlie interrupted, her eyes evaluating the scene as she gestured for me to come back to the chair I'd been in before. A silent sorry exchanged between us. "I think we're ready to rinse out the dye."

Excusing myself from the meddlesome trio, I finished up my appointment, happy with the results.

All that was left was to find Micah. All this talk about him had me craving him.

Who was I kidding?

I was ready to sink into his arms and take up where we left off outside Shear Magic. If there was one thing I was beginning to know about that man, it was that one kiss would never, *ever* be enough.

CHAPTER 10

"Mmmm, that smells delicious!"

Micah came up behind me and placed his hands on either side of me, resting on the kitchen countertop. His breath was soft against my ear, and it was suddenly difficult to concentrate on chopping up the vegetables we'd be having with the steaks he'd be grilling.

Focusing on the knife in my hand, I tried not to moan out loud when his breath was replaced with his mouth. A bolt of desire shot through my body, and a wave of shivers made me squirm a little against him.

If he had even a fraction of an idea about how he affected me, he would probably tease me without mercy. Not that I wouldn't enjoy every blissful second, but with a sharp object in my hand, I couldn't guarantee it wouldn't end up bloody somehow.

"That marinade smells divine," I agreed, taking a small bite out of the green bell pepper sliver before offering him the rest. "My mouth keeps watering every time I take a breath."

"And here I was thinking I was the reason." I didn't need to turn around to know that Micah wore a devilish grin that would've melted me on the spot. For someone who had been reluctant to let me in, Micah wasn't wasting time in showing me exactly how he felt.

Whenever we were together, whether in public or private, he was always reaching for me. And I ate it up like I was starved for affection —a woman thirsty after a lifetime of drought.

"I have one word for you, mister," I retorted, scraping the cutting board clear of bell peppers. All that was left was to slice some tomatoes and dice the cheese, and my salad would be complete.

"And that would be?" He spoke softly because he was too busy nuzzling my neck, leaving trails of blistering heat.

"Holly."

Micah let out a long, exaggerated sigh. "I guess that's my cue to see if the grill is ready."

Surrounded by the cold and snow outside, a small covered patio out back protected the state-of-the-art grill—and its griller—from the weather. He'd only just come inside from turning the gas on before he'd snuggled up behind me.

"Well, you were complaining earlier how hungry you were." I turned around to face him as Micah gave me the room to move. The second I locked eyes with him, he pressed against me again.

There was a hardness now that made me gulp—whether nervously or lustfully, I wasn't quite sure.

His voice was rough and husky. "My appetite has changed. I'm more interested in . . ." And instead of telling me what he wanted, Micah showed me.

There was no tentativeness or shyness about the kiss he leveled me with. It held all the power and determination of a man who had no problem claiming what he wanted. Not that I was in any position to refuse him, as my body softened into him and my arms worked their way up around his neck.

With his fingers in my hair, tugging the back of my head firmly, he totally owned the kiss—setting the pace as his tongue brushed against my mouth. I acted instinctively and parted my lips, moaning the instant his tongue touched mine.

Everything about Micah overwhelmed me in the best possible way.

He made it hard to breathe—to think—to remember that only moments ago I was warning him we had a teenage girl in the house with us. He was both gentle and brazen, giving me just a tiny taste of submission before he took control and dominated the kiss.

I let him.

I encouraged him.

I drowned in him.

It was painfully blissful in the agony he stirred within me, because all I wanted to do was grab him by the hand and take him to his bedroom. We hadn't really talked about it, but as his tongue danced with mine, I was willing to show him that behind every girl was a woman just begging to let loose and indulge in her wildest fantasies.

I wanted to be wild.

I wanted to rock his world.

He set me on a rollercoaster of indescribable emotions that frankly scared the crap out of me, because they felt so new and raw.

The kiss was over way too soon.

Leaning back in to steal one last taste, I stared up at Micah with what felt like stars in my eyes. "Where did that come from?" I sounded all sexy and raspy.

"Just a promise of what's to come." The look he gave me set off a flurry of butterflies inside my stomach. It was one that whispered he was talking about more than just kissing.

We were combustible.

All I could do was grin like a dork, making sure to slap his butt on his way out to the grill.

"My gosh, I thought you two would never stop." Holly peered around the corner from her room. She clutched her stomach like she was in pain and gagged repeatedly. "I thought my eyes might bleed."

I burst out laughing. "Just you wait."

I didn't say anything else. I already knew she had a crush on Austin. If given a chance, I was sure she'd kiss him, too.

"Yeah, but still." Holly walked over to the island counter where I was standing and peered at the salad in the bowl. Before I could stop her or caution her to wait for dinner, she plucked out a cucumber chunk and shoved it into her mouth. "Not where we eat."

With each passing day Micah and I spent together, I also got a chance to get to know his sweet young niece. She had very little memory of her parents, and her uncle had basically raised her. There was no mistaking how much she loved him, and it was endearing to hear her share small story after small story of things he'd done for her growing up.

The tales weren't anything too revealing—other than how totally committed and doting he was. He denied her very little, and in return, Holly showed him a level of respect well beyond her years. She trusted him completely, even when she didn't understand his constant need to move. Holly would follow him to the ends of the earth and jump into space if he asked.

Such devotion was impressive.

"Did you get your homework done?" I asked, changing the subject. That was the other thing I admired about Micah . . . he'd nurtured in Holly an incredible love of reading. Earlier, I'd gotten another chance to look at the shelves of books Holly called her own personal vault of knowledge, and her eclectic tastes were evident in the variety of books I saw.

If she had even the slightest interest in it, chances were she also had a book or two about it.

"Yep. I finished that book about Henry the Eighth you got me!" she answered with excitement. "I'm kinda sad that it's over."

She definitely was a kindred spirit. I had those same feelings— what I called a book hangover. The greater the adventure or tale, the deeper the sadness.

"Quick, tell me what you loved most about it . . . a fact." The tomatoes were finally sliced into fourths and spread out over the top of the lettuce.

She shrugged. "Hmmm, I thought it was interesting that for a man who thought he was popular with the women, he wrote really bad love letters. I guess it was a good thing he was king, otherwise he would've never had a family." Another thing about Holly was, despite her not liking to see her uncle make out, she was a horrible romantic. "But he was also very musical, so maybe that's how he charmed them."

My knife cut through the small block of cheddar. After cubing two strips, I offered them to her before dumping the rest in the salad. "I don't think it really matters what he did. Like you said, he was king. He could do pretty much whatever he wanted."

Before I could say it, Holly spoke. "Well, wasn't that what he was infamous for?"

With my part of the meal completed, I quickly washed my hands at the sink and peered out the window to see how Micah was doing. Judging from his smile, it was time to take out the steaks to him.

"You want to take this outside to your uncle?" I asked, holding the rectangular glassware containing the meat. "I'll finish setting the table if you want to come help after?"

Nodding, Holly took it from me. "I like it when you come over, Sedona. Micah talks to me about what I read, but it's not the same." Her smile was sweet and innocent.

"Well, you know where to find me."

Our conversation came to a halt as Micah came bursting into the kitchen. He was no longer relaxed. Something had lit a fire under him, and his eyes reflected the frenzy.

"Holly. Hide. Now," he barked out his order. "You go with her, Sedona."

Holly didn't argue. She dropped the glassware on the floor, and it shattered on contact, as she rushed out of the room. Sauce slowly started dripping from the fresh meat, a small pool spreading outward.

"What's going on?" I began to ask, but Micah was already halfway out the door.

Calling out over his shoulder, he repeated his demand that I follow Holly. "Don't argue with me. Just do it."

The patio was lit by two overhead light fixtures. As I took a few steps down the stairs and into the backyard, the light began to fade, the sun finally setting. Micah was already moving into the gradual darkness, and ignoring him completely, I chased after him.

"What's going on?" I repeated, running until I finally caught up with him. He was stalking around the perimeter of the house's property, brushing against the solid fence that encased it.

His gaze was constantly scanning his surroundings. If it was at all possible, he seemed larger, more terrifying, more like a battle-hardened warrior than the carefree man who stole kisses earlier.

This time a chill went through me, because this was the same Micah I caught a glimpse of that day he came barging into the store looking for Holly. He carried himself like a man who would kill first and ask questions later—if he even bothered to ask at all. He looked like someone most would cross the street to avoid.

It was alarming how powerful the transformation was.

"Micah!" I called out, expecting him to stop. He didn't.

"Why won't you listen?" There it was—that ever so slight sound of exasperation. It made me wonder how many times he'd had similar conversations with Holly before she responded the way she just had.

His question made me pause, and I also began looking about. The night was quiet with a chill in the air that I was only just now feeling. From the way Micah was vigilantly studying the woods, his pace never slowing as he circled around the house and back to the patio, I knew that this wasn't merely some crazy paranoia on his part.

"Is someone here?" I let out a sigh of relief when I was finally able to join Micah. "Micah?"

"I have a quartz grid around the house. They're specifically spelled to ward against malicious intent and to protect all who reside on the property. Whenever there is a threat lurking by the boundary, the crystals are programmed to alert me immediately." Micah finally looked at me long enough so I could feel his seriousness.

"And they went off?" I asked, already guessing the answer. That would explain his inspection of the property. Something had obviously triggered it. "And?"

I felt like an ass always asking questions, but he didn't always give complete answers.

He nodded. "I won't jeopardize her safety. The second I'm alerted, I act." Her being Holly.

"Are we under attack?" I asked, suddenly feeling sick. "Oh no, I left her alone. I didn't listen to you." I closed my eyes, wishing I could take back my stubborn ignorance. I started back to the house, but Micah reached out and stopped me.

"My wards are strong enough that no one with malicious intent can breach them. Whatever it was that triggered the crystals is outside."

That made this all the more creepy—my beloved woods were now filled with sinister shadows.

"So we're safe?" I repeated as a throbbing headache started blossoming.

That's when it hit me.

"Micah? How many times has this happened? How many times have you given Holly that order?" All I could think about now were the steaks abandoned on the kitchen floor amidst shattered glass. She hadn't even taken the time to carefully place the dish back on the counter before rushing off. Holly had simply dropped everything and obeyed.

"Too many to count."

His confession hurt my heart. It hurt my soul. It made me weep for the kind of vigilance it took to always be that ready to respond—to act automatically without thought. It made me want to pull Holly into my arms and hold her until the world was a safer place. It felt unfair that this was their lifestyle . . . like they were merely pretending to live between each attack.

"Who are you afraid of?" I asked, searching his eyes for a hint. Gently, I cupped the side of his face, hoping that the intimacy of my touch would encourage him to share. "Is someone hunting you?" All I could think of were the mobster movies I watched on television, where someone would witness a murder and have to go into hiding.

His expression turned to one of pain. "Don't ask me that, Sedona. You know I can't tell you. Not because I don't want to, but because the less you know, the safer you are."

"But you're not safe and neither is Holly." I stated it as a fact. After what I'd just witnessed, it was impossible to casually brush it aside.

Speaking of Holly.

I started heading back into the house, and Micah joined me. "Is this all she knows? Please tell me this hasn't been her entire life."

Visions of them bolting into the night with only the clothes on their backs filled my mind. I imagined them moving to new town after new town, always having to look over their shoulders, never trusting a soul.

He tugged me to a stop, my hand in his. "And this is another reason why I didn't want to bring you into our lives. To be with me, to be around Holly, you're also putting yourself in danger. I can't ask you to be so careless with your life."

I could feel him pulling away. I'd finally seen behind the iron curtain where he kept his secrets hidden, and it had scared him. He wasn't even trying to disguise the fear in his eyes as he looked at me.

There was no way I was going to let him retreat.

As we entered the kitchen again, I stopped dead in my tracks and turned around. I was about to do something I vowed I would never do.

I slipped my hand into my pocket and pulled out my phone. "If you can't confide in me, then there's someone I think you should talk to." When he went to interject, I shook my head, determined to get this next part out before I second-guessed myself. "If you truly are in that kind of danger, you're going to need help."

"So who do you suggest?"

Dialing the last number I thought I would, I took a deep breath before answering.

"You need to talk to my aunt."

CHAPTER 11

I couldn't keep from pacing outside the closed door. Every instinct in my body yelled for me to run fast and far, because while I'd been the one to initiate this discussion, I had no idea what was happening inside between my aunt and Micah. From the moment they met, I'd been excluded from the conversation.

I could never tell which way my aunt would spin something, and a niggling feeling whispered that our prior discussion about me using my gifts to uncover his secrets may arise.

The thought of jeopardizing what was growing between us turned my stomach sour. Maybe I should've been honest from the beginning and told him.

I'd tried to talk with him before—to explain that despite what my aunt might say, I hadn't wanted to spy on him. It had been the very last thing I wanted, and I had adamantly refused her.

Yes, the Court used empaths when they needed to discern the intentions of others, but it had never sat well with me. Only under extreme persuasion and duress would I cave to their badgering. Thankfully, they had other empaths they could employ. It was my aunt who relished the opportunity of reminding me where my duty lay.

I had no problem helping and doing my part. It was the uninvited prying into the emotional psyches of people that left a nasty taste in my mouth.

The door handle quickly turned, and the door swung open.

The look on Micah's face was calm and professional. He shook the hand of my aunt, murmuring something to her before stepping out into the hallway.

Perhaps it wasn't so bad, I thought, inwardly sighing with relief.

Perhaps she'd stuck strictly to what I'd shared with her—that Micah may need additional help from the coven in protecting his beloved niece.

That was when he finally turned to me and lowered his guard. Thunder and anger blasted at me so hard that I staggered backward from the force.

His glare was like a lance piercing my soul.

"Sedona," Aunt Millicent said, staring at me over the glasses perched on her nose. "I appreciate you informing me about Mr. Westbrook's needs, and I believe we've reached an appropriate compromise. He has officially registered himself and his niece as permanent residents of Havenwood Falls and kindly shared his intentions of moving here. The coven won't be requiring your services after all."

I couldn't speak even if I wanted to, as the realization hit me like a ton of bricks—there was no way Micah wouldn't understand her meaning. Now I knew the reason why he dropped his guard and let me in. Now I knew why a storm brewed deep inside him.

My mouth flapped open, and I struggled to find the words.

"Thank you, Aunt," I mumbled, regretting that I'd been foolish enough to trust her. They said that family was everything and that there was nothing you couldn't turn to them for. My intentions had been sincere—I'd earnestly believed meeting with her would result in some kind of comfort for Micah. I didn't want him feeling so alone. While I hadn't expected him to share his secrets with everyone, he could believe the coven would step in and join his efforts to protect Holly.

I looked at him, hoping that by some miracle he would stay long enough to listen to me explain. He had to know that I would never spy on him, that the times we'd spent together were sincerely because I wanted to be friends—not because I was my aunt's secret weapon.

His brows furrowed in disappointment and hurt. There was no need for me to press against his walls and judge his emotional status. The truth was plastered across his face with a flashing neon sign over his head.

Any trust we'd established together had been obliterated, and tears began to well in my eyes as I watched the shutters fall inside him. What had started between us was now over—a fleeting moment of happiness. Whatever hopes and dreams I held that maybe, just maybe, he could be the one evaporated in a puff of smoke.

"Were you wanting to talk to me, Sedona?" Aunt Millicient interrupted, her voice filled with arrogant impatience. In that moment, I wished I could blast her far away. I'd confided in her how much Micah was beginning to mean to me, and she'd ignored my feelings and acted in true Millicent fashion—nothing mattered but the coven and its agenda.

I stood staring at Micah, imploring him with my silence to please give me the chance to explain. Words still failed me. All my life, words and sentences had filled every waking moment, but now, I was confounded over what to say.

For a moment, I thought he was also quietly willing me to say something—anything so the ugly truth didn't hang between us. But as each second ticked by, his jawline twitched from the clenching of his teeth.

I knew the precise second when he gave up.

It was also the exact time I found my voice, but it was too late.

"Micah, wait!" I called out as I watched him turn and head toward the exit. I couldn't let him leave like this.

He paused in his tracks, his back still to me. "There's nothing more to say, Miss Mathews."

His use of my last name felt like a dagger in the heart.

Reaching out, I gently grabbed his arm, hoping he would face me.

"It's not what you think! I honestly thought this would help. I didn't want you carrying your burden alone!"

Micah whipped around, his features twisted with anger. "So it's not that you were asked by your aunt to use your gifts on me, to find out why I was here in Havenwood Falls?" When I went to answer, he shrugged off my hand and gestured for me to stop. "All those times I felt you pressing against my wards, trying to read me—it wasn't because you were curious, but because you were working for the coven? All the times you asked me to trust you, to let you in, was any of it true, Sedona? Or was it all a charade . . . a game?"

It was my turn to feel hurt. "Seriously, do you think so little of me that I would do that?"

"Honestly? I don't know what to think right now. All I know is I can't stand here a second longer. I told you I didn't have time for friendship and romance . . . for whatever has been building between us. I was truthful when I said that I wasn't expecting you. I have one mission, Sedona, one task before me, and I allowed myself to become distracted by you."

I could feel what was approaching—the sledgehammer of pain that was swinging fast toward me. Out of desperation, I stepped toward Micah, only to have him retreat farther away.

"Please don't say it," I implored. I didn't care how needy that made me sound. Tears threatened to spill over my cheeks, and I shook my head in denial.

"You've left me no choice. Respect my wishes, Sedona. We can't be friends, and I ask that you don't encourage Holly to come to the bookstore anymore."

I drew in a jagged breath. All while my aunt watched on, like those who slow down as they pass a car accident. The casualty this time was my heart.

"Please." One word. It was all I could utter as my mind raced to find the perfect thing to convince him this was a horrible misunderstanding. The problem, however, was I knew this could've been avoided had I been open with him. Countless conversations flittered through my mind, showing me missed opportunities where I could've broached the topic.

Micah had entered the meeting I'd arranged blind. I'd assumed my aunt would stick strictly to what we'd discussed, and now she'd reduced me to an ass who looked like she'd been hiding something from the man she was dating.

In his eyes, I had betrayed him.

"Sedona," my aunt said. "Let the man leave."

Fury boiled up inside me, and I whipped around to level her with a hateful glare. "Don't you think you've done enough? You were meant to help him, not make things worse. I told you I didn't want to be used as some kind of tool in your arsenal. I refused you when you asked. At no time did I ever agree to spy and pry at your request. Why would you give that impression?" I took another deep breath, my hands shaking at my side.

"I'm not responsible for how others interpret things. Besides—" With a jaunty smirk, she pointed behind me. "He doesn't seem too interested. I would think any man who respected you and held any kind of affection would stick around long enough to hear what you had to say in your defense."

The emotions I had struggled to rein in broke free, and the tears finally fell. "I didn't do anything wrong! You were the one being deceptive! He was someone important to me, and you trampled over everything. Your position with the coven doesn't justify you acting like a . . ." I bit my tongue at the last moment before I hurled at her words that would've disappointed my mother.

"Watch your tone, young lady," Aunt Millicent chastened. "Remember who you're speaking to."

Once upon a time, I admired the woman before me. Part of me had hoped to make her proud, but life had shown me a different path, and I wouldn't be carrying on her legacy any time soon.

"That's the problem. You're the one who's forgotten who she's speaking to." Not waiting for her reply, I shook my head sadly and walked away.

She didn't call out for me to stop.

CHAPTER 12

I tossed the book back onto the counter in disgust.

"I don't know why I bother," I complained, a slight whine in my tone. It was no use. The stories I once loved to escape into had banned me from entering, and I was left trapped in my own reality.

It didn't matter which book I tried, my heart just wasn't in it since last week, when Micah had walked away. He wouldn't answer my calls, and true to his word, Holly had stopped coming to the store. Even Austin was missing her.

"Just give him time, love," Maxwell gently counseled. His usual snark was gone, and in its place was a grandfatherly concern. "If you two are meant to be, just give him time."

"What does that even mean?"

"It means, you working yourself up into a tizzy isn't going to solve the problem. Take a deep breath and show a little faith." For a ghost who often liked to tease, Maxwell's advice was actually sound.

Pity I wasn't done wallowing in my sorrows.

"I guess this is it. I'm officially dubbing myself the Cat Lady of Havenwood Falls. I can be eccentric and kooky and die a spinster." The defeatist tone in my voice was pathetic. Glancing to the side at

Maxwell, I murmured more. "I just really liked him." I let out another frustrated huff.

"Well, I can always go talk to him. Perhaps rough him up and make him see the error of his ways." My friend cracked his knuckles menacingly. I knew that he was trying to cheer me up, but a part of me knew, if given a chance, Maxwell would've been kicking down Micah's door, demanding answers.

I started giggling. "How would he take you seriously if you took a swing and your fist went right through him? I'm grateful for the sentiment, but I think it's best I just do what he says and leave him alone."

I'd gone through our brief argument over and over in my head— viewing it from different perspectives. There was no ignoring the fact he felt betrayed. He'd warned me from the beginning that he didn't have the luxury of letting people close to him and Holly.

"Perhaps, given time . . ." I muttered out loud, staring out across the town square. I could scarcely believe that life was moving on as if nothing was amiss, and meanwhile, my world had been tossed upside down.

Who'd have thought I'd have fallen so quickly for him?

The door jangled as Austin stepped through. He cautiously approached the front counter where I'd been sitting.

"How is it going today?" He eyed me curiously, as if he was an empath too, and was assessing the situation.

He was another person who was worried.

"I'm not falling to pieces, if that's what you're wondering," I retorted with a slight snort. "Relationships end all the time, Austin. Life goes on. It's no big deal." That last part was a lie. It was a big deal, but I wasn't going to give in to the constant temptation of climbing back into bed and forgetting the world for a while. "Besides, we have work to do."

That elicited a loud groan from Austin.

"Then what about my heart?" He staggered forward with his hand over his chest like he was wounded. "I miss Holly and her million questions about everything."

"Again, you're a senior and she's only fourteen years old," I reminded him, sounding like a broken record. Not that it mattered either. Holly was homeschooled, and for all I knew, Micah was planning on leaving Havenwood Falls completely. He had suggested that the last time I saw him, but an insistent feeling inside me whispered to be prepared.

"I know," he blustered, rolling his eyes. "I'm no cradle robber. All I'm saying is she was a great study partner. It's a shame she couldn't keep coming in. I went out to her house the other day, but Micah said she was resting."

At the sound of his name, my insides started whirling about like butterflies. "You did?"

A jumble of questions flickered through my mind. I just couldn't give them voice as the words stumbled before reaching my lips.

Behind Austin, Maxwell's ghostly form reappeared, and he threw me a saddened look. He heard the hope I still felt.

Austin's school messenger bag dropped behind the counter with a heavy thud. "I think it's safe to say you're not the only one moping about."

I slapped his shoulder. "Who's moping?"

Maxwell mouthed the word at the same time Austin answered, "You."

"Well then," I replied, standing up from the counter stool and straightening myself out. "Consider this an intervention." I snatched up one of the flyers Eloise had asked to put in the store. "No more hiding away. I'm going to the psychic fair coming up, and who knows, maybe I'll get my fortune read—figure out why I'm so disastrous in love."

My declaration made the sadness in Maxwell's eyes deepen before he faded away.

"That's the spirit," Austin cheered, a smile returning to his face. "Who knows, maybe Holly will be there, and we can at least convince Micah to let her come back to the bookstore. We were developing a pretty close friendship."

Shrugging my shoulders, I warned him not to get his hopes up. If there was one thing I knew, it was that Micah was unflinching when it came to Holly. He never did share why he was so overly protective, but to me, it didn't really matter.

He wasn't the only stubborn one.

While my mouth said that it was time to move on and there were plenty of guys out there, my heart screamed something different.

He couldn't simply walk in and out of my life like that without some kind of explanation.

It was time to corner him and demand one.

CHAPTER 13

A slight breeze caused the candle's flame to dance, tendrils of potent incense smoke twirling upward.

Callie gripped my hand tighter, staring down at my palm with all the concentration she could muster. The tip of her tongue peeked out between her lips, and it was hard to take her seriously.

"So what do you see, oh powerful swami?" I asked, barely containing my amusement. The annual spring equinox festival was in full swing, and the cold weather didn't deter people from attending in the slightest. It was as if the promise of spring hung heavy around us—blinding us from the presence of residual snow with whisperings of sunshine and warmth.

Havenwood Falls loved to celebrate, and Eloise always organized an incredible Into the Mystic New Age & Psychic Fair. It was one of those opportunities to bring the supernatural community members together with the human ones, and for one day, rejoice in the differences and share gifts otherwise hidden. They said that Halloween was when the veil between the dead and the living was the thinnest, but for me, it was this time of year that held its own brand of mystique.

Usually we had to be careful not to give away our secrets and reveal our true identities. Tonight, however, it was all in jest and for entertainment. It was amazing how humans could suspend disbelief for a few hours in the name of community and charity.

Callie cleared her throat and leaned over closer, her finger tracing over a line on my palm. "You have quite an adventure coming your way." Pausing for a dramatic sigh that was meant to convince me of her authenticity, her voice lowered to a soft rasp. "You will fall madly in love with . . . a carnival ride operator, who will sweep you off your feet. He will win your heart at the top of the Ferris wheel."

I burst into laughter and withdrew my hand. "Impossible. I'm scared of heights."

Rolling my eyes, I crossed my legs and sat back in the chair. If there was anyone in town that I felt I could be close friends with, it was Callie. She ran the local consignment store, a place that I regularly got lost in as I sorted through the many treasures she had. I always teased her that I was tapping into my inner dragon because all I wanted to do was buy everything that caught my eye. Unfortunately, my bank account didn't agree.

Spoilsport.

"You can't argue with me," Callie countered, waving her hand before her like she was beckoning the spirits of her ancestors. "Perhaps I should gaze deep into the crystal ball and see what truths lurk there."

Her long brown hair fell like a curtain over her eyes, and she tucked it behind her ears. Her style was a little more eclectic than mine, but tonight Callie's outfit screamed gypsy fortune teller. Despite the weather, she wore a full-length skirt with assorted beads sewn into patterns in the fabric. Her jade-colored peasant shirt matched her skirt and brought out the green in her eyes. She was such a striking woman, but that wasn't what I liked about her. She had the same quirky personality and sense of humor as I did. She never failed to leave me laughing or smiling.

"Ahhhh, I see it now," she whispered in hushed tones. She waved me to join her peering into the ball. "There is someone. Oh, he's tall, dark, and handsome." Callie fanned herself, all part of the show. "Girl, you're going to fall so hard for this one."

Playing along, I grinned. "Does this stranger come with a name?" In the back of my mind, Micah's name floated to the surface. It brought a hint of sadness that I pushed back down. "How will I recognize him?"

Her gaze flickered over my shoulder to where the festivities were still happening. Each vendor was given a large space to set up in, and she'd chosen to have a canopy-like tent that would keep in the warmth from the portable heater by her feet. What humans didn't know was that the coven had also placed a spell over the fair so that the elements wouldn't ruin the event. So while we all donned our favorite coats and boots and walked around with rosy cheeks, no one completely froze.

It was another perk of living in a supernatural town like Havenwood Falls.

"Something tells me he has a sweet tooth for snow cones." Callie's smirk told me that she was being a little too specific for a reading on my future.

"What?" I asked, already turning about in my seat. My eyes instantly found the meaning behind her comment. Micah was currently talking with Zoey, a resident frost dragon, at her snow cone booth. Most didn't see it, but Zoey made her treats by blowing her cool breath, and she had a way of making anything taste delicious. Holly was standing to the side of him, happily pointing to the different flavor bottles. My lips formed a silent O.

I'd been looking for him all night, anxiously hoping he'd come, yet here he was, and I had a sudden case of nerves.

"I can't, Callie," I confessed, slumping back in my seat as I faced her. "I screwed up and broke his trust. There's really no point falling for someone who doesn't even want to talk to you anymore." A slight quiver filled my voice, and I took a quick breath, praying I wouldn't cry. It was crazy to cry over a guy—no matter how incredible he looked.

Or kissed, my own thoughts betrayed me.

"I don't know what happened, but I know there was a spark of something between you. Why don't you go over and at least try?"

"Did you know a summer on Uranus lasts twenty-one years? Or that it rains diamonds on Jupiter and Saturn?" My cheeks flushed when I realized that instead of sharing how I felt, I'd resorted to my fact-sharing like it was an armor I wore. I rubbed my brow and let out my own sigh. "Sorry, force of habit, I guess."

Sympathy filled Callie's features, and she placed her hand gently over mine. "It doesn't take any kind of magical gift to see that he means a lot to you, Sedona. You can't hide away with your books forever. If he's someone you want, sometimes you have to fight for him . . . fight hard."

"And if he doesn't want to be won?" I asked, chewing on my bottom lip and staring at Micah again. The lights that were hung around the different booths gave the top of his head an angelic glow. My heart ached to go talk to him, to say hello, to say anything. I just didn't know how to speak—how to say the right words.

"Why don't you start with hello, and take it from there." She squeezed my hand affectionately. "Besides, a gypsy demon doesn't lie about such matters. It's not over between you two. Trust me."

I still wasn't convinced as I stooped to the side for my purse. As I opened it up, Callie shook her head and pointed outside. "Consider it a freebie."

Her smile helped banish some of the butterflies causing a ruckus inside my chest.

"I couldn't," I uttered.

"How about you name your firstborn after me, and we'll call it even?" Her teasing remark made me burst out laughing, and Micah looked over to where we were, his gaze searching. When it met with mine, I gulped loudly.

"I can't do this," I murmured, willing my feet to work. "I'm not some heroine in a romance book."

"You're right, you're not. You're Sedona Mathews, badass owner of Shelf Indulgence, and damn it, I'm never wrong about these things, so off you go."

Micah was still standing, staring at me, while Holly began eating the huge red snow cone he'd purchased for her. I'd expected him to disappear into the crowds, but he hadn't. It was as if his feet wouldn't work either, so I threw caution to the wind.

"Wish me luck," I exhaled. "I might be back later to see if your guides know a way to mend a broken heart." My smile was weak, and I knew it.

A *pfft* sound erupted from Callie's mouth, and I took it as a warning to quickly hustle before she took matters into her own hands. Leaving the safety of the softly perfumed tent, I stiffened momentarily as a chill went through me. I approached Zoey's snow cone stand and returned her smile when she asked if I was interested in getting one.

"They're so delicious," Holly gushed, taking another mouthful that painted her lips and tongue a bright red. "I got one called Dragon's Blood."

I could hear her talking, but my gaze hadn't left Micah's. Testing the waters, I stepped closer. "Hey."

For a second I thought he was going to ignore me, but to my great relief, he nodded.

"I wasn't planning on coming tonight, but this one was going a little stir crazy cooped up in the house." He gestured to Holly, who was still trying to tackle the large icy dessert. "I also figured certain eyes would be watching for me to attend like a good community member."

There was a not-so-subtle dig at the coven, my aunt in particular. She was big on participation and looked down on those who chose to live a more reclusive life.

"I think you're fine," I murmured, peering up into his eyes. God, I missed him. "So, how are things?" The moment it came out, I could feel the awkwardness between us blossom. "I haven't seen you in town lately."

The lines about his eyes crinkled as he gently smiled. "I've been busy. I run most of my errands either really early in the morning or late at night." He glanced about, his eyes scanning the nearby groups of people. "And you?"

How could I possibly sum up everything I was feeling into a few succinct words?

I shrugged, deciding to respond as nonchalantly as possible. "I've been okay. Busy, the same as you. The bookstore keeps me occupied." As if to test the Fates, I quickly turned to Holly. "You're missed at the store. Austin mourns his study buddy."

"I'm sure he does," Micah fired back between clenched teeth, the muscle in his jaw twitching. Obviously, some things didn't change.

Holly had a different response. Her eyes grew wide with interest, and she perked right up. It had nothing to do with the sugar coursing through her body, and everything to do with mentioning my teenage employee.

"Do you know if he's here?" Her head whipped back and forth. She craned her neck to see if she could spot him. "No offense, Uncle, but you suck when it comes to helping me."

Micah didn't look upset in the slightest. He was probably gloating over how he'd saved her from the evil clutches of male hormones and lust.

"Holly," he warned, his tone suddenly stern. He shook his head at her, and it did the trick. She closed up and returned to focusing on her treat.

I hated the awkward silence that fell around us like the choking grip of the Grim Reaper. My own emotions bombarded me—anxiety, loneliness, desire, need, hope, and frustration. All I wanted to do was to reach out and touch him, but Micah felt too far away.

Take a risk, a brave part of my psyche urged. *Speak up.*

"Micah," I blurted out roughly. My hand whipped out to take his. I was so terrified of missing the moment—any moment—with him that it felt impossible to hold it all in without screaming. Steadying myself, I briefly closed my eyes. When I opened them back up, Micah was all I could see.

"Please." I squeezed his fingers with mine and searched his face for any hint to what he was feeling. His mouth softened a fraction before he tugged me toward him. I stumbled against him.

"I can hear you better when you're closer." He was staring at me with the intensity of a million suns. Instead of scorching my skin, it warmed me from deep within. "You were saying?"

Staring up into his beautiful blue eyes, I finally found the right words.

CHAPTER 14

*T*here are many types of kisses in the world.

While I was in no way an expert, I knew they held the power to sweep you off your feet, lifting you high into the air, before gently cascading you back like a feather on a breeze. True, it was an extremely romantic ideal that each press of the lips could elicit such pleasure, but for as long as I could remember, I'd hoped against hope that such kisses existed.

I'd read my fair share of books. I lived vicariously through both classic and modern literature—swooning over knights and their princesses. I knew that kisses could reveal an extraordinary range of intimacy, but I also knew that *the* kiss with *the* right person held enough force to decimate them all.

All the legends.

All the myths.

Each and every kiss that had gone before it.

They paled in comparison to the feeling bubbling inside me as Micah cupped my face so carefully, his thumbs brushing back and forth across my skin, his fingers in the hair at the back of my head.

He owned that kiss.

He sealed that kiss.

It held a promise that it wouldn't be the last and that while we had more to discuss, we would face whatever came together.

Micah feathered his mouth over mine again before he pulled away. Slowly, the sounds around us filtered back, and the chill from the air reddened my cheeks.

I could taste him in my mouth—his emotions, so raw and delicious against my tongue. It was a perk of being an empath. I didn't just feel what others felt—I could also taste it.

Forgiveness. Openness. A willingness to try again.

The kiss held more than I'd hoped for.

"Let's get Holly and head home," Micah said, his lips against my temple, his breath grazing across my skin.

"You don't want to get your palm read by Callie? Perhaps she'll give you the winning lottery numbers or something?" I couldn't help the lighthearted teasing or the huge grin on my face. It didn't matter that the town was still covered with snow and that winter was having a hard time relinquishing its control to spring. I was warm all over.

He rolled his eyes as he turned about, looking for Holly, his arm slipping around my shoulder. "I'm feeling pretty lucky." His voice grew faraway, and Micah dropped his arm as fast as he had embraced me. "Why would I . . ." His voice trailed off.

His worry provoked my own. I started looking about, not knowing what was happening. "What is it?"

"Where's Holly?"

Two words, and the happiness that had just been brimming over inside me vanished.

"She was just here. Maybe—" I whipped about and raised onto my tiptoes. "Maybe we embarrassed her with the public display of affection and she's over by one of the stalls, giving us some privacy?"

"She knows not to wander without saying something." Micah didn't bother to hide the concern in his voice. "She wouldn't leave without telling me."

I trailed beside him, trying to convince him that he was worried for nothing. "She's a teenage girl, Micah. She's going to defy your rules and do what she wants. Just take a deep breath. I promise you she's okay. You're going to scare her if you don't calm down."

The look he threw at me spoke volumes. In the time it took for me to give my little spiel, his anxiety had ratcheted up a few notches from worry to full-on warrior mode.

"Micah?" I grabbed his hand to pull him up short. "What aren't you telling me?" When he brushed my question aside and craned his neck to peer over me, I was tempted to punch him in the gut or stomp on his foot. "Hello?"

He must've snapped out of whatever thought had locked him in because he shook his head, and finally answered me.

"You're right," he replied feebly. "She's probably gotten distracted." His nods looked more like he was trying to convince himself than me.

"You know—" I had his complete attention now. "Maybe she headed over to the store to see if Austin was there? He was meant to come tonight after locking up at the end of the day. I haven't seen him yet, so maybe they're together?"

His nodding slowed as sense penetrated his dark thoughts. "How about you head over there now, and I'll check a few places we stopped by tonight? There was a crystal necklace she fancied. Maybe she went there?"

It was good to hear him breathe. The warrior guy he'd briefly morphed into was a little scary. It made me wonder again what kind of supe he was.

I pulled out my phone and glimpsed at the screen. "We'll meet there in fifteen minutes. If either of us runs into any problems, call. Okay?"

I turned up the volume on my phone before pocketing it again. I also had it on the vibration setting, just in case.

His kiss lacked the intensity from earlier as he absentmindedly pecked my cheek.

He was worrying for nothing. Holly was a teenage girl prone to distraction and due a few moments of defiance. He'd find her and scowl, and all would be okay.

This was the beginning of our happily ever after . . . or at least the possibility of one.

Life was perfect-ish.

Damn pesky feeling.

~

"HOLLY?" I called out, dumping my unused keys to the store on the counter. The door being open with lights still blazing was a good sign. She'd probably come searching for Austin, seizing a quick moment to touch base with her friend.

Reaching for my phone so I could call Micah, I chuckled softly to myself. He was such a worrywart. Maybe this would finally convince him to relax the death grip he had over her.

"Austin?" I hollered, wondering if they were in the back storeroom or something. Each step I took, however, felt like I was wading through quicksand with concrete slippers. I shook my head—once, twice, three times sharply. Something was wrong . . . very, very wrong.

Emotions hit me like a ton of bricks and stripped away every defense I'd ever erected. The sensations obliterated all reason until all that was left was fear.

Blinding.

Bile-inducing.

Nauseating.

Fear so powerful that it took me a few seconds to ground myself the best I could as I ran toward the pulsating source. Holly.

"Holly!" I screamed as I entered the storeroom to find her whimpering in the corner, her legs and arms bound, a strip of duct tape stuck over her mouth. Angry tears streamed down her reddened face, and she struggled to break free from her restraints.

A million thoughts flickered through my mind, one being that Micah had been right all along. He had warned me of danger, told me there was a reason he was so guarded. I stumbled to grab hold of my phone, my fingers shaking, barely keeping the device from falling to the ground.

Muffled cries filled my ears.

"Give me a second, Holly," I muttered, abandoning the phone so I could work on the tape cutting into her skin. "Who did this to you?" I stammered, rambling with a slew of questions part of me knew she couldn't possibly answer yet.

Adrenaline coursed through my body as I shook my head once more. Emotions were jumbling over and over in my head, distorting my vision momentarily. The tape failed to give way no matter how gently I tried tugging at it. The last thing I wanted was to rip away her soft skin, but the greater her panic swelled, the more deafening it sounded in my ears.

"I need you to calm down, honey. You're safe now. I promise. Micah's going to be here. I'm trying to get this off you, but I need you to stop fighting me, okay?"

With trembling hands, I cradled Holly's tear-streaked face and looked deeply into her eyes. I pushed out every soothing thought and feeling I could muster, pushing down and past my own terror.

When that didn't work, I reached back around to the chain clasp behind my neck and released the black tourmaline pendant I was wearing. I didn't even think. I simply reattached it back around hers.

Grounding her would ground me.

Placing my palm over it, pressing it against her sweat-drenched skin, I closed my eyes and said a quick spell to help unravel the tape so it wouldn't rip too much of her flesh with it. My heartbeat slowed with hers, and with it, the room became easier to breathe in.

The tape at the corner of her mouth finally gave way, and with a quickly fired apology, I yanked it off. "Better?"

Holly nodded. "I didn't know," she sobbed, her words broken up.

"Where's Austin, Holly? Is he hurt? Did he go get someone?" One more tug, and I had her hands free. Her skin was a mottled red— blotchy, hot, and angry. "I need to call the police . . . Micah . . . I need to make sure whoever did this doesn't come back."

I was rambling, my body still shaking as I pressed the back of my hand against my forehead. I was way out of my league. I'd never been in a situation like this before. Hell, I'd never even had to deal with shoplifters. I'd been blessedly kept from harm's reach my entire life, and nothing had prepared me for the intensity of the adrenaline and shock.

Dragging in a deep breath, I focused on the air filling my lungs. I focused on the feel of the clothes on my body. I focused on the sensation of my heart thudding in my chest. It was a technique I employed whenever I was overstimulated and was a surefire way of finding the balance I needed to act.

I may have been only a fact-wielding bookworm and not some lethal warrior badass, but I wasn't some fainting damsel in distress either. Micah needed me to keep my head about me until he got here.

I stood, moving toward the door. Holly was busy working on the tape around her ankles.

"Hopefully whoever did this was scared off." I was being optimistic, a trait that hadn't failed me in the past.

Austin blasted into the room, knocking me over. "Sedona! You're here! Quick, you need to get down and hide . . . they're back!" A frenetic energy bounced off him, plowing into me.

Wait, wait . . . wait, my inner voice screamed. Something wasn't right.

"You?" I gasped, leaping to my feet in confusion. Instinctively, I stepped in front of Holly, protecting her. "Austin?" I croaked in disbelief.

My gaze dropped to his hands—in the left, Austin held a gun, and in the right, a roll of duct tape.

He raised the weapon to my head, a cynical smirk on his face. Damn, he didn't even look like the high school student I'd taken under my wing and given a job to for the past year. He didn't feel the same either. Austin felt bitter, the taste burning the top of my tongue with its acidity.

"I can't stand another second living here, Sedona. If you knew who we were surrounded by . . . the monsters . . ." Austin's eyes bulged a little in his head as he glanced about nervously, the gun in his hand dipping. "You would've done the same thing if you were looking at failure. I was promised scholarships. I played by all the rules, and then

I get the brush-off. Ask me what happened, Sedona." When I didn't answer fast enough, Austin shook the gun at me angrily before swinging it to aim at Holly. "*Ask. Me.*"

I gestured for Austin to calm down with my hands, hoping to convince him to lower the gun or at least aim it back at me. "What happened, Austin? Tell me? Maybe I can help?"

He shook his head, and beads of sweat flicked from his damp hair. "How do I know you're not one of *them*?"

The way he emphasized *them* made me wonder. Austin was human.

"Did something happen at school?" I took a tentative step away from Holly, forcing him to keep his attention on me. "Did you have a fight? Fail a class?"

I knew he'd been anxious over an exam he had, but I was so used to his normal adolescent neuroses that I tended to tune the overflowing emotions out.

"I was promised a theater scholarship to any university of my choice . . . wherever I wanted to attend around the country. I was told it was all but official, so I didn't bother submitting for any other funding options. They said I didn't have to worry about the financials, and to just focus on my academics and my extracurricular drama workshops. I did everything I was told, but I guess people lie."

I took a bolder step. Austin's face was like thunder, his brow twisted into furrows. My heart hurt for him, because he had talked about nothing else since his counselor had advised him at the beginning of the school year. I guess something had changed.

"Surely there was a mistake. Put the gun down." I took a step toward him, my arm still outstretched. I had never worked so hard at layering my voice with calm, soothing tones. "How about we go in to the high school tomorrow and ask for a meeting?" I was closer now. "This isn't how you solve the problem, however."

"Let me go, Austin, please. Maybe my uncle could help too." Holly's sniffles snapped the distracting spell I'd been weaving.

"Actually, you are my ticket out of here. Imagine my surprise when a stranger pulled me aside, said he worked for someone he called the

Collector, and offered me easy money. All I had to do was answer questions about people around town. The money was crazy good, so of course I jumped all over it. And then he started asking about your uncle and said if I ever saw you, to call him, and he'd make it worth my while."

His laugh bordered on maniacal, his smirk turning into a snarl.

"I don't care that they gave my scholarship to that freak anymore. I don't need it. With the money I'll make delivering you to this Collector guy, I can study anywhere I want in the world."

I was a riot of contradicting emotions. My heart hurt that the young man I'd grown to love was nowhere to be seen in the angry and bitter diatribe Austin was delivering. I wanted to erase away the hurt and promise him I'd find a way to get him to college without reducing him to the gun-wielding attacker he was now.

But that was nothing compared to the word echoing in my head.

Freak.

Somehow, Austin had discovered that it wasn't just humans who lived in Havenwood Falls, and based on his brief description, one obviously stole what he thought was rightfully his.

"You've underestimated my uncle if you think you're going to leave this store!" Holly yelled, her courage kicking in.

"No, I believe that's what I should be saying to you," Austin spat. Desperation drenched his words. "Now get up. We need to go."

Holly's gasp sounded seconds before mine escaped through my lips.

Cocking back his fist, Micah slammed a punch so hard that it lifted Austin off his feet and threw him into the shelves before he crumpled to the ground. The gun skittered across the floor until it came to a stop.

"No. I believe my niece was right the first time."

CHAPTER 15

I was at a loss for words.

The Devil himself couldn't have painted a more formidable and awe-inspiring scene than Micah standing there in all his menacing glory. Electricity rippled off him in tsunami-sized waves as he surveyed the scene before him.

He was breathtaking—magnificent. In all my short life, I didn't think I'd ever seen a man look so incredibly sexy, yet in the next breath look as if he could rip your face off with his teeth. When he said that he took care of his niece and wouldn't allow anyone to place so much as a finger on her, he meant it.

Austin groaned weakly on the ground. Micah had completely incapacitated him. Based on the death glares he was still leveling at someone I'd thought was a friend, he'd let Austin off easy.

"Is everyone okay?" Micah growled, his breathing ragged and chest rising rapidly. He rushed toward Holly, who met him halfway. Her arms were around his waist in the blink of an eye, her face buried into his shirt as she sobbed buckets of tears.

"I'm so sorry, Micah," she repeated, over and over again like a broken record. Her shoulders shuddered as she struggled to control her crying, her small frame dwarfed by his larger one.

"Shh, sweetheart. It's okay. I'm here. This wasn't your fault. He caught me by surprise as well." Micah rubbed Holly's back in a fatherly manner as he cradled her in his arms. "There's nothing you could've done." He glanced over to me, his eyes doing a quick once-over to check I was okay. He relaxed a little once I nodded. It could've been worse than the bruised skin where Holly was bound and a bad case of the shakes.

"How did they find us? We were careful. I promise you, I didn't tell Austin anything!" Holly's sobs had turned into broken words echoed with hiccups.

I came closer and wrapped my arms around them both—enveloping Holly between us. "Who are they?" I whispered, looking cautiously at Austin. "What's going on, Micah? Why did my employee suddenly become a psychotic, gun-wielding kidnapper?"

I didn't know what hurt most—being kept in the dark by Micah or that I had been so blindsided by Austin. I'd become so accustomed to withdrawing inwardly and not using my gifts that I'd totally missed any telltale sign that he had been plotting anything.

"It's a long story," Micah began, placing one more kiss on top of Holly's head. "One I think is overdue. Let me get Holly home, and we can talk." He kicked at Austin's still body. "I'll call Sheriff Kasun while we're on the way."

"Hopefully the police department doesn't have their hands full tonight with the fair going on," I added. I dragged trembling fingers through my hair. My brain was having a difficult time processing the last fifteen minutes.

How did I go from getting my fortune read to this?

Micah took hold of my hand and squeezed it, gently pulling me with him as he guided Holly out into the main floor of the store. I tried not to look up when we passed by shelves. I felt violated—the safe haven I'd created for myself from my inheritance felt confining and defiled. I knew it was just a building and that the real blessing was no one was hurt and Austin's plans had been diverted, but it didn't stop the pain from pressing down on me.

"We'll smudge the store thoroughly," Maxwell offered feebly, his ghostly form barely present. "Don't let this break you, Sedona. You didn't know."

"I should've known!" I exclaimed, forgetting I was the only one who could see my phantom friend. My anger blistered my insides—the rush of changing emotions drowning me. "I'm a god damn empath, and I had no idea!"

"No one's mad at you, sweetheart," Micah comforted, and for the first time since this nightmare started, he wrapped his arms around me.

That's when Holly shocked me.

"I think she's talking to the ghost, Uncle." And she pointed straight at Maxwell. I couldn't tell who was more stunned—me or him.

"You see me?" he said, flustered.

"You see him?" I echoed, my eyes growing wider by the second. "Are you all keeping secrets from me now?"

She'd caught Micah off guard, too. His attention flipped back to her. "See who?"

Holly's smile was so genuine and pure, it made my heart ache. "Well, yeah. When no one introduced him to us, I figured that he was a secret. If there's one thing I know how to do, it's how to keep one."

Maxwell's pale jaw hung open. If it wasn't for what had just happened, I would've relished watching him be so flabbergasted.

"I had no idea." Stroking his mustache, he gestured to Micah. "Can he see me?"

Holly shook her head. "I don't think so. Unless he's being a complete jerk and ignoring you."

All eyes turned to Micah, who looked adorably clueless. "Someone needs to fill me in now. You have a ghost?"

Stifling a yawn, I was partway through saying yes when another one hit. "I guess we have more to talk about than we thought." I turned around and gave my bookstore one more look. "But how about we leave that subject for another day? I'm still trying to wrap my head around this."

It was on the tip of my tongue to complain about the monster headache pounding away like hail on a tin roof when a blinding pain unlike anything I'd ever experienced pierced my body, dropping me instantly to the ground.

"Sedona!" It was Holly I heard screaming, but all I could see was Austin dragging himself out of the storeroom, his now smoking gun beside him.

He shot me. The sentence sounded weird inside my head. *He shot me, and I'm bleeding.*

Fire blazed through me, burning over every nerve until they lay blistered in its wake. I couldn't keep myself standing. No matter how many times I told my brain to move—to do anything—it responded with more agony until all that was left was to close my eyes.

The ground felt hard beneath my body. I'd fallen, but someone was lifting me up.

"Sedona," the voice cried out. It sounded so far away, though. All I knew was that in the maelstrom of intensity, that voice was the only thing tethering me to life.

I'm dying. The thought floated in and then floated out.

"I'm dying," I croaked. That's when the shock set in, and I started to laugh.

"You need to heal her, Micah. There's no time."

Holly. That voice belonged to Holly.

Awareness slowly creeped back in, and the blissful ignorance faded away until all that was left was the harshness of reality.

I was lying in my bookstore.

Austin had tried to kidnap Holly.

Micah had stopped him.

Austin had shot me.

I was now bleeding out in Micah's arms.

"She's right," I answered weakly. "By the time you reach the doctor, it'll be too late."

My blood stained the front of my shirt, and for some sick reason, all I could think was how annoyed I was that my new shirt had been ruined. I'd barely bought it from Callie's Consignments the day before, and it was now destroyed.

Micah placed his hand over the bullet's exit wound. "The coward shot you in the back," he barked, applying pressure.

I winced at the contact, but didn't attempt to move his hand. I couldn't if I tried.

"Heal her!" Holly screamed again. "I don't care if you've kept who you are hidden to protect me. Heal her now, Micah!"

My brain was muddy, but I still tried to understand what she meant. My head lolled to the side as the edges around my vision grew darker.

Micah lowered his lips to my ear, and I savored the warmth of his breath. *Cold.* I was so cold.

"I didn't want you to find out this way, sweetheart. I thought my secrets were more important, and with it being too late to even get Elias here, there's no other choice. Close your eyes." When I didn't, he gently brushed his fingers over my lids and shut them for me. I stiffened at his touch. "Don't be scared. I've got you."

"Elias?" My mouth formed the word but nothing came out.

"I guess you could say he's my brother."

I didn't hear the rest. I couldn't, as the most peaceful, glowing, soothing light filled me. It was everywhere—with no ending or beginning. It penetrated every shadowed corner of my soul, purging away the pain with a different kind of fire.

A healing fire.

A *holy* fire.

"Micah," I cried out, my body arching as I felt that warmth spread relentlessly throughout me. Cells sung with restoration. Wounds healed. Pierced organs rebuilt themselves. It was miraculous, and it all emanated out of Micah and into me.

I didn't want to move or speak. I didn't want to do anything that might break that incredible connection forging out of him and into me. The walls that he had kept so painstakingly erect were nowhere to be found as he let me in and healed me completely.

When it was over, and my weary fingers rested on the ground, my body drenched in sweat, I slowly opened my eyes and gasped.

Micah filled the room.

No, his *wings* filled the room—each illuminating white feather ruffled from being unfurled. I'd had my suspicions about what kind of supernatural creature he was, but never had I guessed he was divine.

"You're beautiful," I murmured as tears filled my eyes. "My gosh, Micah. You are beautiful."

He silenced me with his lips as he lifted me back into his arms. I could barely hear a commotion happening outside as Elias's handsome face came into view.

"I felt you," he said to Micah. "I got here as quickly as I could, so if you want to keep your identity secret still, I suggest you hide yourself before the police arrive, wondering who fired a shot."

Indecision warred in Micah's face. "Can I truly hide my nature now? They're going to want answers." He continued to ignore me, but I caught his gaze darting over to Holly, who now stood with her arms wrapped around her body.

"Blame me. Tell Kasun what happened, but when it comes to healing Sedona, say the Fates were smiling, and I was the first to arrive here."

Micah shook his head firmly. "No. I can't ask that of you."

"True, but I'm offering, and this way you get to disclose to whomever you choose in your own time. Quick." Elias cast a confident look outside, and I envied that he could take this all in stride. I was a mess. "You won't have privacy for much longer. The shifters would've heard the gunfire."

The decision was made with a brisk nod. "Thank you."

Elias reached out and stroked the side of my face. "I'm sorry you were hurt, Sedona. Hang in there. We'll get you home quickly."

Leaving to go meet with the police when they arrived, Elias slapped Micah's back. "Take care of your women."

I tried not to let that rankle as I cozied up to Micah more.

"You're an angel. My angel."

"What I am is a fool."

I didn't get a chance to argue with him. With the angelic powers he held, Micah lulled me into a restful sleep.

CHAPTER 16

"*P*enny for your thoughts."

It was the next day, and despite my feelings from last night, I'd opened up Shelf Indulgence this morning as though nothing had happened. True, I was still ignoring that back storeroom, but —baby steps.

Just like Rome wasn't built in a day, erasing what Austin had tried to do would take some time.

I said I was working, but honestly, that was me sitting at the front counter, staring out into the town square. I could see Maxwell hovering in my peripheral vision, but I didn't have anything to say.

Apparently, he was tired of my silence.

"It was my fault." It was the thought among many that had stuck to the forefront of my mind all day. When Maxwell didn't answer or argue back, I slowly looked at him. "I should've known."

"You're being too hard on yourself. You're young, and your gifts are young."

I had no idea how long he'd been rehearsing that, but I wasn't buying any of it. To me, they were merely words—excuses—we said when we hoped to placate someone. The blame had to fall somewhere, and as the empath, I couldn't deny I felt responsible.

"Austin was my employee. I introduced him to Holly. Do you know how often we talked about her together . . . speculating about why Micah was so secretive? All this time, under my nose, and I had no clue."

"Do you actively read people?" He gave me a stern look. I was surprised he didn't pair it with pointing one of his pale slender fingers at me. "Are you all-wise, all-knowing?"

"Maxwell!" I exclaimed, slamming my hand down hard on the counter. "I. Should've. Known." There was no way I was going to budge. I'd had all night to stew in my insecurities and musings.

"Fine." He threw his hands up in frustration. "Then you need to share the blame and guilt around. Don't be greedy, Sedona. We all deserve a huge serving of self-loathing this morning."

I snorted in disbelief. "How do you figure that?"

I clicked on the computer's keyboard, bringing the screen to life. Letters and numbers filled the brightness, but it all looked like a jumbled mess to me.

Maybe I should've stayed home like Micah had suggested.

"This entire town knew or at least has seen Austin, and no one noticed he was unhappy. How many times does your aunt come in here to harass you? A high-ranking coven member, and she didn't sense anything either. You didn't see her nefarious deeds alarm go off, did you?" He was being silly, but I saw his point.

Relenting a fraction, I took in a deep breath. "I promised them both things would be okay."

That was what stung the most. I had convinced Micah I was someone safe to befriend and then look what happened—our world had exploded in gun smoke and violence.

That's when the real reason buried under all my guilt surfaced.

"He's going to leave, Maxwell. I saw it as plain as day when he was healing me. When he arrived in Havenwood Falls, he vowed that at the first sign of trouble, he would leave immediately with Holly. He would never risk her safety again, once he knew a place was too dangerous. And before you say it, do you honestly think I'm the best person to tell him to stay?"

"Yes, Sedona! Can't you see he feels something for you?" His eyes lit up with passionate fervor. "And before you argue with me, a man can tell these things about another man. You stole his heart."

"But that was before, and this is now," I fired back. "Too much has happened."

"You didn't see his face when you were shot, or the blatant fear that threatened to break him when you said you were dying. I'm telling you, Sedona, quit being stubborn and go talk to him."

Micah and I had agreed to meet later, after I convinced him I'd be okay. Holly was his priority, and from what he'd shared, she was still pretty shaken up.

"Face it, Maxwell. My spinster status is still secure. He won't be staying."

Tuning him out, I stared back out the window.

And I need to somehow let him go.

I MUST'VE DOZED OFF, because the next thing I was aware of was Maxwell yelling loudly to rouse me.

"Sedona, get up now!"

Chills skated over my sleep-dazed senses as I cracked open an eye.

"Sorry, I guess we should just lock up for the day and go home. I'm not much use here anyway." I'd tried all day to keep busy with orders and light dusting, but my heart just wasn't in it. Untouched books sat beside me at the front counter. Even the delicious treats from the bakery that I sold to customers with their purchases remained uneaten.

"He was leaving Havenwood Falls, but I convinced him to wait long enough to say goodbye." Maxwell was as solid as I'd ever seen him, his hands fidgeting with agitation. "You don't have much time, though. Hurry."

A million thoughts raced through my mind. "What? Micah was here?" Stretching out the tight kink in my neck, I looked about. "Why didn't he wake me?"

"Sedona," Maxwell exclaimed again, sounding like he wanted to shake me. "There's no time to explain."

And with that, my ghost friend disappeared—only to reappear outside the bookstore in the middle of the town square. A loud squawk went up us he startled a few people taking a brisk walk through the center.

Once he knew I'd seen him, Maxwell popped back in, amused by the astonished expression I wore.

"You left!" I gaped. "How the heck did you do that?"

He reached for my hand. It breezed through my own. Some habits, no matter how long ago used, were still hard to break.

"We don't have time, Sedona. Please. For once, do what you're told and go to Micah's home. He told me he could hang around for an hour—no more. Go, or you'll miss out on your chance to tell him how you feel."

The world felt like it was crashing down around me—sounds blurring until all I could hear was the truth. Micah wasn't even going to tell me what had happened. He wasn't even giving me the courtesy of saying goodbye before he and Holly disappeared.

When he'd taken me home the night before, it was with the understanding that once we were all better rested, we would talk about everything. Any question I had, and I had many, would be rewarded with answers.

Yet here was the painful truth—I hadn't even warranted that level of respect.

"It's better this way," I replied, rapidly shutting down each and every feeling I had. I didn't want to feel anymore. I was done being empathic, and I was over opening my heart, only to feel it break. When Maxwell tried to argue, I dug in deeper. "His life is not his own. If it was, I truly believe he would've come himself."

I picked up a chocolate mint brownie I'd placed on a plate earlier, but didn't take a bite. I crumbled the treat between my fingertips instead, making a mess.

All I could see, however, were all those precious seconds and moments of possibilities—all the what-ifs that could've been mine and Micah's.

"Are you seriously going to spout that bullshit to me?" The corner of Maxwell's mustache twitched as he began chastising me.

"Do you really think anything I could say to him will make a difference? It's not like he's been forthright with anything other than his reluctance in being more social."

"I watched you all these years, Sedona. Witnessed your loneliness and struggles with being empathic. Micah wasn't the only one keeping others at arm's length. What does it say that a beautiful young woman's two closest friends are a stubborn old ghost and a three-legged cat? Somewhere along the way, you got hurt . . . whether from other people's thoughtlessness or unresolved grief over your parents' deaths. You keep to yourself and surround yourself with other people's stories." In a grand gesture, Maxwell waved his hands about to the various shelves that lined the store. "Here is one irrefutable fact for you, Sedona . . . there is no greater story than the one you write yourself. Your tales and your adventures."

He was giving quite the impassioned speech, and I half wondered how long he'd been storing it away for the perfect opportunity. Holding my head in my hands, elbows crooked on the counter, I searched my heart until all I could do was whisper.

"What if I tell him to stay and he leaves anyway?" I'd finally given voice to the real fear hiding behind my bullheadedness. "What if he was never mine to ask?"

"Isn't that what life and love is all about? I'm not saying you have to be madly in love with him, but aren't you even the slightest bit curious? Go. You'll regret it if you don't." Maxwell's features softened, and his gaze filled with tenderness. "Besides, I barely tolerate the cat you have now. I can't imagine the chaos here if you added more felines to the mix."

I started laughing. "I love you, Maxwell. Thank you." Pushing the chair back and grabbing my coat, I wrapped a thick woolen scarf around my neck and tugged a beanie on my head. "What's life without a little risk?"

It may have been the lighting, but I thought a hint of tears glistened in his eyes. "It's what makes all the darkness and uncertainty worth it, sweet girl. Now go and don't return without him."

I didn't even bother replying, locking the store up behind me, before rushing toward Micah's home. The paths were a little icy and slick, but that didn't stop me.

I had no idea what I was going to say when we were face-to-face.

Perhaps words weren't needed.

Maybe it was time to lay it all bare with nowhere to hide.

CHAPTER 17

*H*e was standing in the backyard, overlooking the fence that provided a barrier to the beautiful rich forest of Colorado. All around him, melted snowdrops fell from nearby pines, the air crisp and cool.

I was sure he could hear me approaching as the snow crunched beneath my feet. It wasn't until I was right behind him that he spoke to acknowledge me.

Micah looked exhausted, and his Adam's apple bobbed slightly as he swallowed. "He said you'd come."

Every instinct I had told me to touch him—to somehow convince him that whatever dark thoughts he was having, it would be okay because we could face it together. The words felt like lies, however, because we both knew that it hadn't mattered in the end. Someone had found them, and used Austin to try to hurt Holly.

"I'm still not sure how Maxwell left the store. As long as I've known him, he's been like a permanent fixture. I just assumed he was destined to haunt the place forever." My hand reached out, only to fall short. Micah didn't move closer, either.

"I'm not going to lie. He scared the crap out of me when he

suddenly appeared out of nowhere, but I guess he had a lot on his mind that needed to be spoken."

He still hadn't looked at me.

"You'll get used to him. Maxwell can be rather long-winded when he chooses to." I trailed over to a small path of thawed ground, smiling at the brave little flower trying its hardest to thrive in the frost. "It's amazing how resilient we can be when we have to." It was a random kind of thought that simply fell out. I crouched over and gingerly stroked the pretty purple petals.

"But it would be better to never be placed in that situation to begin with," Micah countered. Even though I'd been musing about nature and the coming of each new season, he was referring to something much closer to home.

"Do you honestly believe that? That life should be as easy as possible with little opposition?"

When he turned to answer, the familiar Micah I'd first met stood looking down at me. Gone was the man I'd seen heal me—love in his eyes, wings unfurled at his back. There had been nothing separating us last night, and now he'd returned to being tight-lipped and shut off.

He shrugged. "I don't know what I believe anymore." Removing his hands from his heavy black coat, Micah helped me stand. "I wasn't lying when I said I wasn't expecting you. I just also know that they will never stop coming for her."

By her, he meant Holly.

"You can't keep running, though, Micah. I'm not saying you have to settle down and live the rest of your life out in Havenwood Falls, but sooner or later, you're going to run out of places to hide. Wouldn't it be better to make a stand where you will at least be surrounded by the support of friends?"

"Are you volunteering for that position, Sedona? Are you ready to die for me and Holly?" Pain filled his face, the first true emotion he'd let show. I wanted to comfort him, cradle his cheek with my hand while we tried to work things out. There were so many things I wanted to say and do, but I didn't.

Damn if my fear wasn't still there.

"I'd be a liar if I said last night wasn't an eye opener. I'm not arguing that with you at all. You told me things could get dangerous, and they did. I just don't think you necessarily have to do it alone. Aren't you tired of always being strong?"

This time I did lightly rest my hand on his arm, and he didn't shrug it off.

"I am old, Sedona. I have existed from almost the beginning of time, and I've experienced so much ugliness in this world. It doesn't matter the time or people—humanity can be cruel with its thirst for power and greed. I never questioned my duty as an angel—a sentinel of mankind. I protect at all costs." He tilted his head to the side, catching my gaze. "I also destroy at all costs. My life was never truly my own, because I was only ever viewed as a weapon."

"But?" He hadn't said it, but I knew one was coming. There was always a 'but' that marked those moments when everything changed, paths diverted, and lives altered.

"And then there was Holly."

Micah shoved his hands back in his pockets, and with his gaze now held by some invisible thing in the distance, he lowered his voice to a hushed tone.

"She's special. She has . . . gifts . . . abilities that could have a profound impact on the world as we know it. And just like me . . . in the wrong hands . . . she could be a weapon of mass destruction."

My mind raced as it flickered through all the different powers and types of supernatural creatures that existed. None of them really screamed the sweet, naïve, fourteen-year-old girl I'd come to know.

"Holly?" I questioned, confused. I cast a backward glance to the house. "She seems so . . ."

Micah barked out a brusque laugh. "Normal?" I nodded quickly. I wanted to pry and ask what she was, but Micah beat me to it. "She's a fledgling oracle who's still trying to understand and learn to use her gifts. In time, she will have the ability to predict situations of great importance and shape them either to the benefit of all or to destruction, if the wrong people control her. With her approaching powers, she could level civilizations, undoing them with a few syllables. She's a weapon that should only ever be wielded when all other hope is lost."

"So you were assigned to protect her?" That made the most sense to me, because it was exactly what I'd been watching him do from the moment I'd met him. It was actually one of those endearing qualities I'd admired of his.

His next words chilled me to my core. "No, I was ordered to destroy her. She is such a wild card that the powers that be deemed it safer to have her killed than risk those with evil intentions using her."

It was my turn to laugh, mine coming out more strangled than his. "And it's not evil to kill a child?"

My voice rang out, and it startled some nesting birds in the trees. Their wings flapping through the air afforded us a temporary moment to pause and breathe. I was only beginning to catch a tiny glimpse into the secrets Micah held, and I already felt like I was drowning.

"It wasn't my position to question my superiors. I was ordered to take her from her home and dispose of her like she—" His voice cracked under heavy emotion. It revealed that despite what he'd said, Micah had grown to love his young charge, and the thought of harming even a hair on her head was utterly abhorrent. "Like she was chattel."

"But something changed," I encouraged, hoping to keep him talking. I tightened the coat around me with the hope of staving off the cold air. There was no way I was moving until I'd heard everything he was willing to share.

Micah snapped out of whatever he was seeing in his mind's eye and approached me once more. Tucking a stray hair back beneath the hem of the beanie, he studied my features until his gaze finally rested on mine. "I looked in her eyes, and I knew that not only would I give my life for her, but that I would spend the rest of my days roaming the earth in order to keep her hidden."

"Micah?" I whispered, feeling completely mesmerized by his confession.

"Sedona," he answered. "It's the same way I feel as I look at you now."

A loud breath escaped from my mouth as his new admission registered. "But you'll still leave."

A stray tear dropped down over his cheek—one single lonely tear that held all the emotions he kept bottled up.

"Because my duty to her trumps what I feel for you. If I stay, there is the very real risk I will lose you both." Before I could say anything, he shook his head, and dug a small velvet pouch from his pocket. "So before we have to leave, there's something I want you to have . . . need you to have. It's the only way I can walk away knowing you'll be okay."

With nimble fingers, he undid the loose knot, and slowly withdrew a beautiful silver chain, but it wasn't the idea of jewelry that made me gasp out loud or my hand instantly cover my mouth.

Hanging from the chain was a silver-filigreed vial that contained an ethereal, glowing substance that seemed to pulse with energy and life.

"Promise me you'll wear this always, Sedona. It's not a lot, but it's enough of my grace to heal you should anyone come looking for us once we're gone. I couldn't bear leaving you defenseless."

My fingers touched the vial, and the liquid responded to my touch. The emotions emanating from it were identical to the glorious feeling of peace and love from last night.

"Your grace." I was completely in awe. "I can't accept this."

I held it back out to him—half hoping he wouldn't take it, because if this was all I could have of him, I would cherish it until my last breath.

"I wish I were a different man. I wish we had met under different circumstances, but we are who we are." He took a step back. He was already distancing himself from me.

Something Maxwell had said inserted itself into my thoughts.

He'd asked me whether Micah was worth fighting for, whether telling him how I felt was worth the risk of possible rejection.

That answer was now a resounding yes!

"We are who we are," I finally said, dropping all of my own insecurities and boundaries. This could possibly be the most vulnerable we might ever be, and it was time to lay it all bare. "I can't predict the future like Holly, and I'm sure as heck no divine creature. My name is Sedona Mathews, and I'm an empath who still has so much to learn. I'm going to make mistakes. I don't have any special survival skills to offer. All I have is me and my capacity to love with everything I have."

And that's when I realized it was bigger than that—larger than just him and me.

"And this is Havenwood Falls. We may have our secrets and flaws, but we are also fiercely protective of our own. Hurt one of us, and you hurt us all. Stay with me. Stay here with us all. Let the town help you protect Holly. No one wants to hurt a child. You might be surprised to find yourself surrounded by others who are equally ready to face the future and the unseen."

Another thought surfaced. "And Micah? Holly isn't the only one here in town with these kinds of powers, so knowing that, don't you think we're better equipped to help?"

"There's more to who Holly is . . . more to who her father is that makes her a target to anyone privy to that knowledge."

I opened my mouth to question him about it, but Micah immediately gestured that he wasn't ready to divulge that particular secret. "It's a secret that I will guard to the death, and even then, there is no force under Heaven that would make me utter those truths."

I knew better than to press the issue. I was simply grateful he'd opened up enough to let me catch a glimpse of what he was dealing with. It was an incredible burden, and one I would figure out how I could best help him carry.

"I'm not suggesting you talk with my aunt again." That little admission caused a smile to curl the edges of his mouth, a soft chuckle rumbling within him. "But there are other coven members who you can talk to. Members of the Court. Someone . . . anyone. All you need to do is ask. We can face this together. You will have the support you need."

"I can't ask that of you or of strangers." He kept shaking his head, but I didn't let that deter me from speaking my truth.

"You don't have to ask, Micah. Don't you see that? I've grown to love Holly, and given a chance, the town will too. You just need to let us in." My hands now lay on his chest, my fingers over his heart. "You just have to give us a chance."

We stood there quietly as the sky began to darken. Neither of us spoke, and it was difficult not holding my breath because my insides were churning with nerves.

Micah's slow grin was like an elixir on my soul. "Did you know that someone sold the air guitar they played at a Bon Jovi concert for five dollars and fifty cents on eBay?"

"Is that so?" I smiled, cocking my eyebrows.

Shivers shot through me as Micah trailed his finger over my cheek. "I figured if I'm going to stick around, I'd better come up with my own source of knowledge. Can't let you have all the fun." His soft chuckle warmed my insides.

"I can't promise what tomorrow holds," I said, and I tightened my grip on the front of his coat. "But we'll face it together."

"Is that so?" Micah brushed his lips over mine, and I felt my body relax.

"That's a fact." Then without waiting, I pulled him in and claimed his mouth, kissing him with everything I had.

Life might not get any easier, and dark days may be headed directly toward us, but in that moment the only truth that mattered was this . . .

Strange things happen in Havenwood Falls, but this is our life.

Oh, and angels are amazing kissers.

Watch for *Addicted to You*, the continuing story of Sedona, Micah, and Holly, coming early 2019.

WE HOPE you enjoyed this story in the Havenwood Falls series featuring a variety of supernatural creatures. The series is a collaborative effort by multiple authors.

Books in the main Havenwood Falls series:

Forget You Not by Kristie Cook
Old Wounds by Susan Burdorf
Fate, Love & Loyalty by E.J. Fechenda
Covetousness by Randi Cooley Wilson
The Winged & the Wicked by T.V. Hahn & Kristie Cook
Alpha's Queen by Lila Felix
Ink & Fire by R.K. Ryals
Lose You Not by Kristie Cook
Tragic Ink by Heather Hildenbrand
Nowhere to Hide by Belinda Boring
Flames Among the Frost by Amy Hale
Rock Me Gently by Susan Burdorf (May 2018)
From the Embers by Amy Miles (June 2018)

More books releasing on a monthly basis

Also try the YA line, Havenwood Falls High.

Subscribe to our reader group and receive free stories and more!

IMMERSE yourself in the world of Havenwood Falls and stay up to date on news and announcements at www.HavenwoodFalls.com. Join our reader group, Havenwood Falls Book Club, on Facebook at https://www.facebook.com/groups/HavenwoodFallsBookClub/

ABOUT THE AUTHOR

International and #1 Multi-Genre Bestselling Author Belinda Boring is known to many readers as the Queen of Swoon and also the Queen of Cliffhangers. Her Mystic Wolves series has topped many charts along with receiving several awards and nominations such as Paranormal Book of the Year, Best Debut Book, and being in the Top 3 Best Rated on Amazon. With additional titles like Bittersweet Melody, Bittersweet Symphony, Enchanted Hearts, Loving Liberty, and Broken Promises, it's easy to see why readers are captivated by this swoon-worthy author!

Facebook: https://www.facebook.com/pages/Belinda-Boring-Author/200626723318915

Twitter: https://twitter.com/BelindaBoring

Instagram: https://www.instagram.com/BelindaBoring

Website: http://www.belindaboringauthor.com

Pinterest: http://pinterest.com/belindaboring/

Amazon Author Page: http://www.amazon.com/Belinda-Boring/e/B005C1IRFC/ref=sr_tc_2_0?qid=1384912397&sr=8-2-ent

Newsletter link: https://docs.google.com/forms/d/e/1FAIpQLSfGcIfO_GUFrNkUP_B-ZM4xvNb662E75dKmvn6WVvKeXEVyfg/viewform

ACKNOWLEDGMENTS

I can't begin to tell you just how excited I am to be part of the incredible Havenwood Falls world! A huge thank you to Kristie Cook and all my fellow authors for letting me be part of the team. You guys are so inspiring, and I'm 100% serious when I say we need to move to this town ASAP. #itsreal2us

As with every project, there's a supportive crew of people who surround me:

To my author coach Jessica Gibson—not only are you one of my bestest friends, but you also understand what's needed when I squirrel hardcore and go off on a tangent. Thanks for keeping me on task and sane through all the crazy. #stuckwithme4life

To my beta readers: Stephanie Krause, Lisa Markson, Julie Engle, Jane Elizabeth Stahl, and Cindy Mayberry—I appreciate you all so much! Thank you for being so excited about Micah and Sedona. Your feedback and love have been such a blessing! #swoonaddicts

To three amazing readers: Brenda Anderson, Amber Jones, and Jade Hakin—I hope you enjoy seeing the facts you entered the giveaway with! Thanks for all your support to not just me, but all the authors within this amazing series. Muah! #seeyouatthenextparty

To Laura Benedict, Susan McCray, and Michelle Boyes—you guys definitely put up with my crazy! Thank you for the many hours you listen to me bounce ideas off you and talk on and on and on about Micah and Sedona. Words can't describe how much I love you! #ioweyoubigtime

Last, but never, ever least, my own personal muse and soul mate, Mark—we did it! We survived the year of HELL and this story is the celebration of it. You are why I write romance and why I love all things swoony. You are in every hero I write and YOU, my darling BFF, will always be my happily ever after. #abazillionkisses4you

Thank you to everyone who purchases this book and gives Micah and Sedona a chance. Thank you for loving Havenwood Falls as much as I do. Whenever you're in town, make sure you stop by Shelf Indulgence and say hello . . . you are always welcome!

Much love,

Belinda #dare2fly

~ A Havenwood Falls New Adult Novella ~

Havenwood Falls

Flames Among the Frost

Amy Hale

AN EXCERPT

Flames Among the Frost (**A Havenwood Falls Novella) by Amy Hale**

Jetta Mills has felt stifled most of her life. She's a rebellious creative who's had to bend to her father's will, as well as the rules of her hometown, Havenwood Falls. Needing a break from it all, she skips town for an adventure far from the smothering influences she's used to. Unfortunately, trouble always has a way of finding Jetta, and she quickly learns that the best place for a frost dragon shifter such as herself is back within the warded borders of home.

When Conrad Monroe is hired to find a thief and bring her back to face justice, the trail leads him to the Colorado mountains and the path of Jetta Mills. She's gorgeous, talented, and a whole lot of trouble. He doesn't know what he's getting into with Jetta and the town she calls home. Jetta has no idea that Conrad has quite a few secrets of his own.

Jetta's seeking real freedom while Conrad's planning to lock her away. But sparks fly between the two as the line between deceit and truth quickly becomes blurred. When the smoke clears, the truth may be the only real path to redemption.

FLAMES AMONG THE FROST

AN EXCERPT

I'd be lying if I said I'd never imagined myself in jail. I'd always been a hot mess with a talent for getting in way over my head. I'd never considered myself a bad person, but I was certainly no angel either. I always ran with the wrong crowd, said the wrong things, dressed the wrong way, and generally pissed off my father by merely existing. Lawrence Mills had been making my life miserable for years, although if you'd asked him, I'm sure he'd have told you the same about me. Despite my love for the rest of my family, I had to escape him. Which, in a roundabout way, was why my ass was going numb as I sat on a cold concrete bench in a six-by-eight cell.

"Damn," I muttered as I adjusted my position. "Hey assholes," I yelled, "are cushions against your religion or something? I can't feel my legs anymore."

I didn't expect an answer. It'd been six hours since I'd been arrested, and outside of my being booked, no one had spoken a word to me. My roommate, Frankie Hopkins, told me she'd be here to bail me out, but I'd yet to see her.

I stood and stretched, hoping to bring some of the feeling back into my limbs. The bland, gray cell was chilly, but actually the perfect temperature for someone like me—a frost dragon shifter. We generally preferred the cold to the heat. I guess when your roots traced back to Iceland, loving the frigid temperatures made sense. It still pissed me off, though. The jackwads didn't even offer me a damn blanket. I think they hoped I would freeze. If so, the joke was on them.

The large metal door at the end of the hall opened, and I listened as footsteps approached. A uniformed officer and Frankie appeared on the other side of the bars. Her tall slender frame, shoulder-length red curls, and blue eyes were a welcome sight after hours of staring at the same cinderblock walls.

"About time," I growled, as the officer unlocked the door. His name tag read Barnes.

"You're free to go, Ms. Mills." Officer Barnes's expression appeared as if those words were painful to push past his lips.

I looked at Frankie, and she smiled. I shoved past them both and stalked down the hall to collect my personal items. The lady behind the window slid a paper bag toward me, and I inspected the contents. I grabbed the pen attached to the clipboard and signed to verify everything was there. Frankie held my jacket open, and I pushed my arms through before stuffing the bag into my pocket.

"May I go now?" I asked with more than a little disgust in my voice.

She nodded. Without another word, I walked to the main doors, Frankie on my heels. I pushed one door open, turned to face the officers standing in the lobby, and flipped them off. "Thanks for nothing."

Frankie rolled her eyes as she shut the door behind us. "Is it really the best strategy to piss off the cops who just arrested you?"

"Are you kidding me?" I glared at her. "Was I supposed to thank them for falsely arresting me, handling me like a piece of meat, and then ignoring me for hours?"

"Of course not," replied Frankie, "but being a bitch isn't going to help anything."

"But . . . I'm so good at it. It'd be a shame to waste my talents."

Frankie put one perfectly manicured hand on her hip. "And it wasn't exactly a false arrest. You did break into that safe, right?"

I didn't know how to explain what had happened. Partially admitting to the altered version of events would make more sense to her than the truth ever would.

"The item I was after belongs to me. I didn't want any of his other shit." I grimaced as I searched for her car in the now dark parking lot. "Thanks for bailing me out."

"Oh . . ." Frankie's voice was hesitant. "I didn't actually bail you out."

My eyebrows rose. "So, how'd you spring me?"

"It was Brandt. I talked him into dropping the charges." She looked nervous.

I felt my temperature rise. I shook my head as I found the nearest wall and leaned against it. As my eyes closed, I saw large claws, scales, and reptilian irises flash in my mind.

"Damn it, no!" I shouted in frustration.

Frankie placed a hand on my arm. "I'm sorry, Jetta, but I couldn't come up with the cash. I didn't know what else to do! I promise it'll work out. Brandt said he'd forgive everything that has happened. That's better than a bail bond, court, and a record, right?"

Frankie didn't understand that, while I was really pissed at her for working out a deal with Brandt on my behalf, the "no" was not about her negotiations. I was commanding my inner dragon to stay back. Being a shifter could be amazing at times, but this was not the time or place to let the beast come out to play. Anytime I felt threatened or upset, she tried to push through and take over. I couldn't allow that. Not again. I wasn't back home in Havenwood Falls anymore, where stuff like that was somewhat normal. This was Atlanta, and supernatural creatures of any kind were still considered part of myth and legend. My kind wasn't welcome in the human world.

I opened my eyes and released a heavy sigh. "So, what did you promise him?"

I quickly walked to her car, not waiting to see if she was following.

Frankie's heels clicked as she ran to catch up. "Not much. Just that you'd give him a chance."

"Oh hell, Frankie," I shouted.

"C'mon, just one dinner. Let him attempt to wine and dine you one more time. Enjoy an expensive meal, then brush him off and move on." She spoke as if her plan was simple, but she didn't know Brandt like I did. She didn't know I'd already been down that road.

"No one walks away from Brandt Sawyer if he feels he's owed something. It's why I'm in this mess to begin with." I frowned. "And now you're in the middle of it, too." I pushed my hands through my hair, still caught off guard by the length since having extensions put in. "Damn it!" I banged my fist on top of her car.

She unlocked the car, and we both climbed inside. "Stop being so dramatic. You act like you're dealing with a mobster or something."

I looked at her and wondered how she could live in such a big city all her life and still be so sheltered. "He pretty much is. He'll use our friendship against me."

"Oh shush." She started the car. "He's an arrogant, rich club owner, and your boss, but I highly doubt he's fitting anyone with cement shoes in his spare time." She rolled her eyes as she pulled out of the parking lot. "I know I haven't known you for long, but your paranoia has gotten really bad lately."

I shook my head. "It's not paranoia. The man is insane. He—" I cut myself off before I let my secrets slip. Frankie didn't need to know all the dirty details about my evening with Brandt. Or the reason it all went to hell. "Let's go home. I'm tired."

She nodded and steered us toward our apartment. We drove the rest of the way in silence, but once inside, I made a beeline for my whiskey stash. I opened the bottle, poured a healthy amount in a tumbler, and downed it in one swallow.

"It's gonna be one of those nights, huh," Frankie stated in a flat voice. She wasn't a fan of my drinking, but I'd made it clear from the beginning that I had vices and those vices would move in with me. Another perk of being a dragon—or con depending how you looked at it—it took a lot of alcohol to get us shit-faced. Thankfully I had a well-stocked bar.

"Yep," I muttered. "It's absolutely gonna be one of those nights." I poured another glass and threw it back, letting the comforting burn slide down my throat. "Do we have mac and cheese? I'm starving. Getting arrested makes a girl hungry."

Frankie jerked her thumb in the direction of the kitchen. "Cabinet."

I nodded and strolled the few short steps it took to travel from our living area to the kitchen, the whiskey bottle my constant companion.

THE ALARM CLOCK screamed in my ears. I rolled over and glared at the blue glowing digits. Seven a.m. wasn't terribly early, but it felt that way when you'd consumed all the alcohol in the house. I slammed my fist down on top, knocking the clock to the floor.

"Shiiiiiit," I moaned loudly as I rolled over. My mouth felt like I'd swallowed a distillery. All I wanted to do was go back to sleep, but I really needed to run errands before rehearsals that afternoon. *Rehearsals! Work!* I bolted upright in bed as my mind reeled with the events of the previous night. Brandt. Our fight. The safe. Jail.

I couldn't stay here, not now. I slid from the bed and pulled my suitcase out from underneath. Tossing it on the bed, I unzipped it and made a beeline for the dresser. Without care or organization, I dumped the contents of my drawers into the suitcase, followed by my clothes in the closet. I had to sit on the lid to zip it shut, but after no small amount of effort, I managed to force it closed.

"I need to get dressed," I muttered as I realized I'd just packed everything. Out of the corner of my eye, I saw the clothes I'd worn the previous evening. Frowning, I looked them over. They were wrinkled, but even worse was the blood on the right sleeve and back of my shirt. I wasn't sure if all that blood was mine. Some of it may have belonged to Brandt. Both of us were injured the night before. Anger seethed beneath the surface. I had to take care of this problem before it became impossible to correct.

PURCHASE *FLAMES Among the Frost* where books are sold.